AN AI

Ethan Frome

Edith Wharton

GLOBE FEARON
EDUCATIONAL PUBLISHER
PARAMUS, NEW JERSEY

Paramount Publishing

Executive Editor: Barbara Levadi
Senior Editor: Bernice Golden
Assistant Editor: Roger Weisman
Adapter: Nancy Gorrell
Art Director: Nancy Sharkey
Cover and Interior Illustrations: Ed Tadiello
Production Editor: Linda Greenberg
Electronic Systems Specialist: José López
Marketing Manager: Sandra Hutchison

ISBN: 0-835-90855-0

Printed in the United States of America
1 2 3 4 5 6 7 8 9 10 99 98 97 96 95 94

GLOBE FEARON
EDUCATIONAL PUBLISHER
PARAMUS, NEW JERSEY

Paramount Publishing

CONTENTS

ABOUT THE AUTHOR

Edith Wharton was born Edith Jones in 1862 in New York City. She came from a well-to-do family. She was educated at home by tutors and in Europe. She married Edward Wharton when she was 23 and he was 36. They lived in New York City and Lenox, Massachusetts. There, she gathered ideas for her story of Ethan Frome.

The Whartons were happy in the first years of their married life. They traveled to Europe, and in 1907, they moved to France. In 1911, Edith Wharton published *Ethan Frome*. It was an immediate success. As her fame as a writer grew, her husband's mental health became worse and worse. He suffered a nervous breakdown in 1910. They were divorced in 1913 after 28 years of marriage.

Edith Wharton continued writing essays, short stories, and novels. *The Age of Innocence* (1920) earned her a Pulitzer Prize for literature. She died of a stroke in 1937 and was buried in her beloved France.

PREFACE

Ethan Frome (1911) is regarded as a masterpiece of short fiction. Although it was written almost one hundred years ago, it raises important questions for readers today. *Ethan Frome* is a timeless story of a man whose desire for happiness conflicts with his sense of responsibility. It is a story of love, loneliness, desperation, poverty, sickness, and, above all else, "moments of decision."

ADAPTER'S NOTE

In preparing this edition of *Ethan Frome*, we have kept closely to Edith Wharton's original novel. Every attempt has been made to keep the spirit and voice of her style. We have kept the natural dialogue of Wharton's characters. We have shortened many of the author's sentences and paragraphs. However, none of the basic story has been left out. Certain words that reflect the life and times of early twentieth-century New England have been kept. They are explained in footnotes if clues to their meanings are not provided in the story.

Dear Reader,

This is the first letter I have ever written to the readers of my stories. But in the case of *Ethan Frome*, I think it is important to tell you something of why I wrote the story and how I wrote it.

I wrote the story about a small village in New England that I call Starkfield. I wanted to write something about New England life because I lived for a time in Lenox, Massachusetts, with my husband, Edward Wharton. To me, New England was a harsh and beautiful land. There were sweet fern, mountain trees, and beautiful, clear skies in the summer. There were also cold, lonely, dark days and wild snowstorms in the winter. Mostly, I wanted to write about the quiet and simple people I knew. To me, they were like rocks, half-hidden in the soil, hard and silent. In *Ethan Frome*, I try to uncover these "hidden" people. I want you to get to know something about their bleak and lonely lives, too.

The problem before me was that I had to tell about Ethan Frome 24 years after the tragic events of the story. My character, Ethan, was too quiet and silent a man to tell his own story, and each of the other characters only knew bits and pieces of what really happened. So I decided, instead, to let an outsider, a visitor to Starkfield, tell Ethan's story. This person, the narrator, comes to Starkfield as part of his engineering work. One day, he sees Ethan leaving the post office. He becomes curious about him. He tries to put together Ethan's story by talking to some of the villagers. In the Prologue, you learn about Ethan as the narrator learns about him. He wonders what happened to Ethan. If I am a good storyteller, you will wonder, too.

Edith Wharton

Prologue

I had the story, bit by bit, from various people, and each time it was a different story.

If you know Starkfield, Massachusetts, you know the post office. If you know the post office, you must have seen Ethan Frome. Every day, he would drive up to it and drop the reins of his hollow-backed bay.[1] Then he would drag himself across the brick pavement to the white front columns. If you saw all of this, you must have asked yourself who he was.

It was there that, several years ago, I saw him for the first time. The sight of him startled me. Even then, he was the most striking figure in Starkfield. Yet, he was a ruin of a man. It was not so much his great height which marked him. Many in Starkfield were tall. It was the careless, powerful look he had in spite of his lameness. When he walked, he stopped after each step like the jerk of a chain. There was a bleak look in his face which seemed to say "stay away." He was so stiff and grizzled that I took him for an old man. I was surprised to hear that he was not more than fifty-two. I heard this from Harmon Gow, who drove the stage between Bettsbridge and Starkfield. He knew everything about the families on his line.

"He's looked that way ever since he had his smash-up. That's twenty-four years ago, come next February," Harmon told me.

I gathered from Harmon that the "smash-up" had caused the red gash across Ethan's forehead. It had so shortened and warped his right side that it was hard

---

1. **bay** reddish-brown horse

1

for him to take the few steps from his buggy to the post office window.

He used to drive in from his farm every day about noon. That was just when I was fetching my mail. I often passed him on the porch. He seldom received anything but a copy of the *Bettsbridge Eagle*. He would put the newspaper into his sagging pocket without a glance. Sometimes, the postmaster would hand him an envelope addressed to Mrs. Zenobia—or Mrs. Zeena—Frome. The envelope was usually from some medicine company. He would pocket this, too. Then he would turn away with a silent nod to the postmaster.

Everyone in Starkfield knew him, but almost no one talked to him. On the rare moments that one of the older men stopped to have a word, Ethan would listen quietly. Then he would climb stiffly into his buggy. He would gather up the reins in his left hand and drive slowly away in the direction of his farm.

"It was a pretty bad smash-up?" I questioned Harmon as I watched Frome drive away.

"Worst kind. Would have killed most men. But the Fromes are tough. Ethan'll likely touch a hundred."

"Good God!" I exclaimed. "*That* man touch a hundred? He looks as if he was dead and in hell now!"

Harmon paused a moment. "Guess he's been in Starkfield too many winters. Most of the smart ones get away."

"Why didn't he?"

"Somebody had to stay and care for the folks. First his father—then his mother—then his wife, Zeena."

"And then the smash-up?"

Harmon chuckled bitterly. "Then he *had* to stay."

Though Harmon told the tale as far as he could, there were gaps between his facts. I knew even then the deeper meaning of the story was in those gaps. I could not stop wondering about Ethan and about what Harmon had said: "Guess he's been in Starkfield too many winters."

Before my own time there was up, I had learned to know what Harmon's words meant. I had been sent up by my employers on a job with the big powerhouse at Corbury Junction. Because of a long carpenter's strike, I found myself stuck at Starkfield for the best part of the winter. It was the nearest spot, and I soon got used to the grim life.

December days were crystal clear, but when I'd been there a little longer, I saw long stretches of sunless cold. The storms of February pitched white tents of snow all over the village. By March, when Starkfield finally gave in like a tired cavalry,[2] I began to understand why winters there were so much like a battle. Harmon's words came back to me: "Most of the smart ones get away." I wondered: What stopped a man like Ethan Frome from leaving?

During my stay at Starkfield, I lived with a middle-aged widow known as Mrs. Ned Hale and her mother. Mrs. Hale's father had been the village lawyer. His house, "lawyer Varnum's house," was the largest mansion in the village. The house stood at one end of the main street. From its small-paned windows, I could see the Norway spruces in front and the slim, white steeple of the village church. Though the Varnums were no longer wealthy, Mrs. Hale did what she could to preserve a certain dignity in keeping with her pale old-fashioned house.

In her "best parlor," I listened every evening to her tales of Starkfield. I had great hopes of getting from

---

2. **cavalry** group of soldiers on horseback

her the missing facts of Ethan Frome's story. But she would only mutter, in a low voice, "Yes, I knew them both . . . It was awful . . . "

So I put my questions once again to Harmon Gow. He told me that Ruth Varnum, who was now Mrs. Hale, had been friends with all of them in her younger days. "She was the first one to see them after they was picked up following the smash-up. It happened right below her house," Harmon said, "just 'bout the time that she got engaged to Ned Hale. I guess she just can't bear to talk about it. She's had troubles enough of her own."

Everyone in Starkfield had troubles enough of their own, yet all agreed that Ethan had the most. But no one could explain to me the look in his face. Neither poverty nor physical suffering could have put it there. I might have been content with the story pieced together from all these hints if I had not met the man himself.

It all happened because Denis Eady's horses fell ill during a local epidemic.[3] Eady was the rich Irish grocer who owned a livery[4] stable. He had agreed to drive me over to Corbury Flats each day so I could pick up my train for the Junction.

Harmon suggested that Ethan Frome might be glad to drive me over.

"Ethan Frome? But I've never spoken to him. Why on earth should he put himself out for me?" I questioned Harmon.

Harmon's answer surprised me still more. "I don't know as he would. But I know he wouldn't be sorry to earn a dollar. That Frome farm was always 'bout as

3. **epidemic** a disease that spreads rapidly
4. **livery** the keeping of horses and vehicles for hire

bare as a milkpan when the cat's been 'round. And you know what one of them old mills is worth nowadays." I had been told that Frome was poor. I knew that his sawmill and the farm barely brought him enough to keep his household going through the winter. But I had not thought him to be in such want.

"Even when Ethan could work from sun-up to dark, his folks ate up most everything," Harmon said. "First, his father got hurt out haying and went soft in the brain. He gave away money like Bible texts before he died. Then his mother got queer with loneliness and dragged along for years, weak as a baby. His wife, Zeena, she's always been the greatest hand at doctoring in the county. Sickness and trouble. That's what Ethan's had on his plate ever since the first helping."

The next morning, when I looked out, I saw the hollow-backed bay between the Varnum spruces. Ethan was waiting for me in the sleigh. He threw back the worn bearskin and made room for me at his side. After that, he drove me every day to Corbury Flats. On my return, he drove me back through the icy night to Starkfield. He always drove in silence, never turning his face to mine. But there was nothing unfriendly in his silence. He seemed to be part of the lonely, frozen landscape about us. I began to realize what Harmon meant by the cold of too many Starkfield winters.

Only twice did we get close to conversation. One time, I spoke of an engineering job that I had the previous year in Florida. To my surprise, Frome said suddenly, "Yes, I was down there once, and for a long while after, I could call up the sight of it in winter. But now it's all snowed under." Then he said no more.

Another day, when getting into my train at the Flats, I couldn't find the science book I had carried with me to read. I thought no more about it until I got into the sleigh that evening. I saw the book in Frome's hand.

"I found it after you were gone," he said.

I put the book into my pocket, and we became silent again. But as we crawled up the long hill to Starkfield ridge, I saw that he had turned his face to mine. "There were things in that book that I didn't know the first word about," he said.

"Does that sort of thing interest you?" I asked.

"It used to," he said.

I told him I'd be glad to lend him the book. He paused for a moment. Then he said, "Thank you. I'll take it."

I hoped the book would help us to talk together. But at our next meeting, he made no mention of the book. Something in his past or present way of living drove him too deeply into himself. He became silent once again, and our talk remained one-sided.

Frome drove me over to the Flats daily for about one week. Then, one morning, I looked out the window to see a thick snowfall. The drifts looked like white waves against the garden fence. The storm must have been going on all night. By the sight of the snow, I knew my train would be late, but I never doubted that Frome would come. His sleigh glided up through the snow like a ghost behind a thick veil of white haze.

"The railroad's blocked by a freight train stuck in a drift," he explained. "I'll take you straight to the Junction by the shortest way." He pointed with his horse whip to School House Hill.

"To the Junction in this storm? Why, it's a good ten miles!"

"The bay can do it if you give him time. You said you had some business there this afternoon. I'll see you get there."

He said it so quietly that I could only answer: "You're doing me the biggest favor."

"That's all right," he replied as we drove off into the stinging whiteness.

Near the schoolhouse, we took a fork in the road that led us past Frome's sawmill. It looked dead enough. Its cluster of sheds sagged under their white load of snow. Frome did not even turn his head as we drove by. About a mile down the road, we came to an orchard of starved apple trees. Beyond the orchard lay a field or two lost under drifts of snow. Then we saw one of those lonely New England farmhouses that make the landscape even lonelier.

"That's my place," said Frome, with a sideways jerk of his lame elbow. I did not know what to answer. The snow had stopped. In the flash of sunlight, I could see the house in all its ugliness. The thin wooden walls, under their worn coat of paint, seemed to shiver in the wind.

"The house was bigger in my father's time. I had to take down the 'L' a while back," Frome continued. I then saw the sad and stunted look of the house. It was partly due to the loss of what is known in New England as the "L." These additions connected the main house to the woodshed and cow barn. Without the "L," Frome's house seemed to reflect his own shrunken body.

As we turned onto the Corbury road, the snow began to fall again. We could no longer see the house. Frome fell silent. This time, the wind did not stop with the snow. It sprang up with the force of a gale.[5] The horse was as good as Frome's word, and we pushed on to the Junction through the wild white scene.

---

5. **gale** very strong wind

I finished my business as quickly as possible. We set out for Starkfield with a good chance of getting there for supper. But at sunset, the storm began again, bringing an early nightfall. The small ray of light from Frome's lantern was soon lost in the smothering snow. Even the horse lost his sense of direction. I persuaded Frome to let me get out of the sleigh and walk along through the snow at the horse's side. In this way, we struggled for another mile or two. At last, Frome said, "That's my gate down yonder."

The last stretch had been the hardest part of the way. The bitter cold and the heavy going had nearly knocked the wind out of me. I could feel the horse's side ticking like a clock under my hand.

"Look here, Frome," I said. "There's no use in your going any farther." I was thinking that I would walk the rest of the way.

But Frome interrupted me. "You shouldn't go any farther either," he said. "There's been about enough of this for anybody."

I understood that he was offering me a night's shelter at the farm. Without answering, I turned into the gate at his side and followed him to the barn. There, I helped him unharness and bed down the tired horse.

"This way," he called to me over his shoulder.

Staggering along, I almost fell into one of the deep drifts against the front of the house. Frome scrambled up the slippery steps of the porch. Then he lifted his lantern, found the latch, and opened the door. I went after him into a low, unlit passage. On our right, a line of light marked the door of a room. Behind the door, I heard the droning[6] voice of a woman complaining.

---

6. **droning** low, dull, monotonous

Frome stamped on the worn mat to shake the snow from his boots. He set his lantern on a kitchen chair. It was the only furniture in the hall. Then he opened the door.

"Come in," he said, and as he spoke, the droning voice grew still. . . .

It was that night that I found the clue to Ethan Frome, and began to put together this vision of his story. . . .

Chapter 1

The village lay under two feet of snow with drifts at the windy corners. In a sky the color of iron, the points of the Big Dipper[1] hung like icicles. Young Ethan Frome walked at a quick pace along the empty street. He passed the bank and Lawyer Varnum's house, with the two black Norway spruces at the gate. Opposite the Varnum gate, the church reared its slim, white steeple. As the young man walked toward it, he could see many fresh tracks leading to the basement door. A line of sleighs waited with heavily blanketed horses under a nearby shed.

The night was perfectly still. The air was so dry and pure that it gave little feeling of cold. At this unexpected moment, an image came into his mind. Four or five years earlier, he recalled, he had taken a year's course at Worcester College. He had worked in the laboratory with a friendly professor of science. His father's death and the troubles following it had put an end to Ethan's studies. Though he had not learned enough to use in his work, his studies had fed his mind. They had made him aware of the world of nature around him.

At the end of the village, he paused before the darkened church. He stood there a moment breathing quickly, looking up and down the street. Not another figure moved. The pitch of the Corbury road below Lawyer Varnum's spruces was the favorite coasting[2]

---

1. **Big Dipper** a group of stars arranged in the form of a long-handled cup
2. **coasting** sledding

ground of Starkfield. On clear evenings, the church corner rang till late with the shouts of coasters. But tonight, not a sled darkened the whiteness of the snow. The hush of midnight lay on the village. All those awake were gathered behind the church windows. There, dance music flowed with the bands of yellow light.

The young Ethan went down the slope toward the basement door. He edged his way among the shadows to the nearest window. Holding back his body, he stretched his neck to get a glimpse of the room. The floor was filled with girls and young men. By this time, the music had stopped. The musicians—a fiddler and the young lady who played the organ on Sundays—were refreshing themselves with pie and ice cream. The guests were preparing to leave. Some even had their wraps on.

Suddenly, a young man with black hair jumped into the middle of the floor and clapped his hands. The musicians hurried back to their instruments as the dancers fell into line along both sides of the room. A lively young man grabbed a girl who had already tied a cherry-colored scarf about her head. He led her up to the end of the floor and whirled her down its length to the tune of a Virginia reel.[3]

Frome's heart was beating fast. He had been straining for a glimpse of the dark head under the cherry-colored scarf. The man leading the reel danced well, and his partner caught his spirit. As she passed down the line, the scarf flew off her head. At each turn, Frome caught sight of her laughing, panting lips and the dark eyes which seemed the only points in a maze of flying lines.

---

3. **Virginia reel** an American country dance where couples face each other in two lines

The dancers were going faster and faster. The musicians, to keep up with them, played their instruments like jockeys lashing their horses on the homestretch. Yet, it seemed to the young man at the window that the reel would never end. Now and then, he turned his eyes from the girl's face to that of her partner, Denis Eady. He was the son of Michael Eady, the Irish grocer, whose new brick store had given Starkfield its first example of "smart" business. His son seemed likely to follow in his father's steps. He applied the same "smartness" to win over the girls in Starkfield. Ethan Frome had never liked him, but now he was angry. It was strange that the girl did not seem aware of Eady's boldness. She lifted her face to his and dropped her hands into his without seeming to feel the offense of his look and touch.

Frome was in the habit of walking into Starkfield to fetch home his wife's cousin, Mattie Silver. She went there on the rare evenings when some chance of fun drew her to the village. Mattie had come from Stamford to act as her cousin Zeena's helper. Because Mattie worked without pay, Zeena thought it best to let her have a few nights out so that she would not feel too lonely.

At first, Ethan did not like having to travel the extra two miles to the village and back after a hard day on the farm. But soon, he had reached the point of wishing that Starkfield might give all its nights to merrymaking.

Mattie Silver had lived under his roof for a year. From early morning till they met at supper, he had many chances to see her. Yet, he liked best the moments when, her arm in his, they walked back through the night to the farm. He had liked the girl from the first day. When he had driven over to the

Flats to meet her, she smiled and waved to him from the train, crying out, "You must be Ethan!"

The coming to his house of a bit of hopeful young life was like the lighting of a fire on a cold hearth. The girl was more than the bright and helpful creature he had hoped for. She had an eye to see and an ear to hear. He could show her things and tell her things. It was during their night walks back to the farm that he felt most clearly the sweetness of this sharing. He had always been more aware than others of the beauty of nature. Before Mattie, the feeling had remained inside him as a silent ache. He had not known if anyone else in the world felt as he did. Now, he knew that one other soul trembled with the same touch of wonder. That soul was at his side, living under his roof and eating his bread.

To Mattie he could say, "That's Orion down yonder. The big fellow to the right is Aldebaran; and the bunch of little stars, like bees swarming, they're the Pleiades."[4] It pleased him to see Mattie's wonder at his knowledge. There were other feelings which drew them together with a shock of silent joy. Together, they could share the cold red of sunset behind the winter hills or the blue shadows of hemlocks on sunlit snow. Once, she said to him, looking upward at the sky, "It looks just as if it was painted!" It seemed then to Ethan that words had at last been found to speak his secret soul.

As he stood in the darkness outside the church, these memories came back to him with a sadness of things gone. Watching Mattie whirl down the floor from hand to hand, he wondered how he could ever

---

4. **Pleiades** in Greek mythology, a group of stars named for the seven daughters of Atlas

have thought that his dull talk interested her. To him, who was never happy except when he was with her, her gaiety seemed open to everyone. When she saw him, her face always looked like a window that had caught the sunset. Now she lifted that same face to the dancers. He even noticed movements he had thought she kept only for him.

The sight made him unhappy, and his unhappiness made him fearful. His wife had never shown any jealousy of Mattie. But lately she had grumbled over Mattie's housework. Zeena had always been what Starkfield called "sickly." If she were really so ill, Frome had to admit, she needed more help.

Mattie had no skill for housekeeping. She was quick to learn but forgetful and dreamy. At first, she was so awkward that he could not help laughing at her. But she laughed with him, and that made them better friends. He did his best to help her by getting up earlier than usual to light the kitchen fire. He neglected the mill so that he might help her about the house during the day. He even crept down on Saturday nights to scrub the kitchen floor after the women had gone to bed. One day, Zeena saw him cleaning. She turned away silently with one of her odd looks.

Lately, there had been other signs of her disfavor of Mattie. One cold winter morning, as Ethan dressed in the dark, he had heard Zeena speak from the bed behind him.

"The doctor don't want me to be left without somebody to do for me," she said in her flat whine.

He had thought her to be asleep. The sound of her voice had startled him. He turned and looked at her where she lay under the dark calico quilt. Her high-boned face seemed gray against the whiteness of the pillow.

"Somebody to do for you?" he repeated.

"If you say you can't afford a hired girl when Mattie goes."

Frome turned away again, taking up his razor.

"Why on earth should Mattie go?"

"Well, when she gets married, I mean," his wife's voice came from behind him.

"Oh, she'd never leave us as long as you needed her," he said, scraping hard at his chin.

"I wouldn't ever have it said that I stood in the way of a poor girl like Mattie marrying a smart fellow like Denis Eady," Zeena answered.

Ethan glared at his face in the glass. He threw his head back to draw the razor from ear to chin.

"And the doctor don't want I should to be left without anybody," Zeena continued. "He wanted me to speak to you about a girl he's heard about, that might come—"

Ethan laid down his razor and straightened himself with a laugh.

"Denis Eady! If that's all, I guess there's no such hurry to look 'round for a girl."

"Well, I'd like to talk to you about it," said Zeena stubbornly.

He was getting into his clothes. "All right. But I haven't got the time now. I'm late as it is," he replied. He held his old silver watch to the candle.

Zeena watched him in silence while he pulled his suspenders over his shoulders and jerked his arms into his coat. Then, as he went toward the door, she suddenly spoke. "I guess you're always late, now that you shave every morning."

Those words frightened him more than any talk of Denis Eady. It was a fact that since Mattie Silver's coming, he had taken to shaving every day. His wife always seemed to be asleep when he left her side in the winter darkness. He had stupidly assumed that she would not notice any change in his looks. Zeena's way of letting things happen without talking about them made him nervous. Weeks later, she would hint at them in passing. She always let him know that she hadn't missed a thing.

Lately, however, there had been no room in his thoughts for such slight fears. Zeena herself, a heavy burden, had faded in his thoughts. All his life was lived in the sight and sound of Mattie Silver. He could no longer think of its being otherwise. But now, as he stood outside the church and saw Mattie spinning down the floor with Denis Eady, Zeena's talk clouded his brain. . . .

Chapter 2

As the dancers poured out of the hall, Frome hid behind a door and watched them. First, the villagers climbed the slope to the main street. Then the country neighbors packed themselves slowly into the sleighs under the shed.

"Ain't you riding, Mattie?" A woman's voice called back from the shed. Ethan's heart gave a jump. He couldn't see her, but he could hear. "Mercy no! Not on such a night."

She was there, then, close to him. There was only a thin board between them. In another moment, she would step forth into the night. A wave of shyness held him back against the wall. He stood there in silence. She came out alone and paused within a few yards of him. She was almost the last to leave the hall. She stood looking about as if wondering why he did not show himself. Then a man approached.

"Gentleman friend not come? Say, Matt, I got the old man's cutter."[1]

Frome heard the girl's voice. "What on earth is your father's cutter doing down there?"

"Why, waiting for us to take a ride. I got the colt, too. I kind of knew I'd want to take a ride tonight." Denis Eady said this in a bragging voice.

The girl seemed to wait. She let Denis Eady lead

---

1. **cutter** a small sleigh, usually pulled by one horse

out the horse and climb into the cutter. She watched
him fling back the bearskin to make room for her at
his side. Then, in one swift motion, she turned around
and darted up the slope toward the church.

"Goodbye! Hope you have a lovely ride!" She called
back to him over her shoulder. Denis laughed and
raced the horse alongside her.

"Come along! Get in quick! It's slippery as thunder
on this turn," he cried. He leaned over to reach out a
hand to her.

She laughed back at him. "Goodnight! I'm not getting in."

By this time, Frome could no longer hear them. He
saw Eady jump from the cutter and go toward the girl.
He held the reins over one arm while he tried to slip
the other arm through hers. She managed to get away.
Frome's heart trembled back to safety. A moment
later, he heard the jingle of sleigh bells as Denis Eady
drove off.

In the black shade of the Varnum spruces, Ethan
caught up with her. She turned with a quick "Oh!"

"Think I'd forgotten you, Matt?" he asked.

She answered seriously, "I thought maybe you
couldn't come back for me."

"Couldn't? What on earth could stop me?"

"I knew Zeena wasn't feeling any too good today."

"Oh, she went to bed long ago." He paused. "Then
you meant to walk home all alone?"

"Oh, I ain't afraid!" she laughed.

They stood together in the gloom of the spruces
under the stars. Finally, he asked another question
that was on his mind.

"If you thought I hadn't come, why didn't you ride
back with Denis Eady?"

"Why, where *were* you? How did you know? I never saw you!"

Her wonder and his laughter ran together like brooks in a spring thaw. Ethan had the sense that he had done something quite clever.

"Come along," he said with pride.

He slipped an arm through hers, as Denis Eady had tried to do. Neither of them moved. It was so dark under the spruces that he could barely see the shape of her head beside his shoulder. He longed to stoop down and rub his cheek against her scarf. He would have liked to stand there with her all night in the blackness. She moved forward a step or two. Then she paused again above the dip of the Corbury road. Its icy slope looked like a mirror scratched by the runners of sleds.

"There was a whole lot of them coasting before the moon set," she said.

"Would you like to come in and coast with them some night?" he asked.

"Oh, *would* you, Ethan? It would be lovely!"

"We'll come tomorrow if there's a moon," he promised.

She stopped, pressing closer to his side. "Ned Hale and Ruth Varnum almost ran into the big elm at the bottom. We were all sure they were killed." Her shiver ran down his arm. "Wouldn't it have been awful? They're so happy since they got engaged."

"Oh, Ned ain't much at steering. I guess I can take you down all right!" He was "talking big." When she said "They're so happy," it sounded to Ethan as if she had been thinking of herself and him.

"The elm *is* dangerous, though. It ought to be cut down," Mattie said firmly.

"Would you be afraid of it with me?" Ethan asked.

"I told you I ain't the kind to be afraid." She tossed her head back. Then suddenly she began to walk with quick steps.

Ethan's mood changed. The fact that he had no right to show his feelings made him aware of her every look and tone. They walked up School House Hill in silence till they reached the lane leading to the sawmill.

Then Ethan spoke up. "You'd have found me right off if you hadn't gone back to have that last reel with Denis." He could not say the name without feeling the muscles in his throat stiffen.

"Why, Ethan, how could I tell you were there?"

"I suppose what folks say is true," he said instead of answering her question.

"Why, what do folks say?"

"It's natural enough you should be leaving us," he stumbled on.

"Is that what they say? Or do you mean that Zeena ain't happy with me anymore?" Her voice broke.

Their arms had slipped apart, and they stood still.

"I know I ain't as smart as I ought to be. There's lots of things a hired girl could do that are still hard for me. I haven't got much strength in my arms. But sometimes, I can tell Zeena ain't satisfied, and yet I don't know why."

She turned on him suddenly with anger. "You ought to tell me, Ethan Frome! You ought to! Unless *you* want me to go, too."

Unless he wanted her to go, too! If only he could tell her how much he wanted her to stay. Then the heavens would melt and rain down sweetness. But he could only say, "Come along."

They walked on in silence through the blackness of the hemlock lane. There, Ethan's sawmill stood out through the night. The path led them to an open clearing, gray and lonely under the stars. The night was so still. They heard the frozen snow crackle under their feet. Suddenly, a snowy branch crashed far off in the woods. It sounded like a gunshot. Mattie shrank closer to Ethan.

At last, they saw Ethan's gate. The sense that their walk was over made Ethan speak up.

"Then you don't want to leave us, Matt?"

He had to stoop his head to hear her whisper, "Where would I go if I did?"

The answer sent a pain through him, but the tone of her voice filled him with joy. He forgot what else he had meant to say. He pressed her against him so closely that he could feel her warmth in his veins.

"You ain't crying, are you, Matt?"

"Of course I'm not."

As they turned in at the gate, they passed the Frome graveyard. It was enclosed by a low fence under the shaded trees. Ethan look at the gravestones slanted at crazy angles through the snow. For years, they had seemed to make fun of him. "We never got away—how should you?" seemed to be written on every headstone. Whenever he went in or out of his gate, he thought bitterly, "I shall just go on living here till I join them." But now, with Mattie, all desire for change left him. The sight of the graveyard gave him a warm sense of home.

"I guess we'll never let you go, Matt," he whispered, as though the dead would help him to keep her. Then he thought to himself: "Mattie and I will always go on living here together. And someday she'll lie there beside me."

Ethan thought of this vision as they climbed the hill to the house. He was never so happy as when he could dream of being with Mattie. They walked on in the snow as if they were floating on a summer stream.

Zeena always went to bed as soon as she had her supper. The windows of the house were dark. A dead cucumber vine dangled from the porch. It reminded Ethan of a crepe[2] streamer tied to the door for a death. The thought flashed through Ethan's brain. "If it was there for Zeena—" He pictured his wife lying in their bedroom asleep, her mouth slightly open, her false teeth in a glass by the bed. . . .

They walked around to the back of the house. Zeena always left the key to the kitchen door under the mat. He stooped down and felt for the key.

"It's not there!" he said with a start. They strained to see through the icy darkness.

"Maybe she's forgotten it," Mattie said trembling. But they both knew it was not like Zeena to forget.

"It might have fallen in the snow," Mattie said.

A wild thought came to Ethan. What if tramps had been there? What if . . .

He was still kneeling when his eyes caught a faint ray of light beneath the door. Who could be stirring in that silent house? Then the door opened, and he saw his wife.

She stood tall and angular[3] against the dark background of the kitchen. One hand clutched a quilt around her flat breast, while the other held a lamp.

---

2. **crepe** a thin fabric, usually of silk, with a wrinkled surface
3. **angular** bony and gaunt; sharp, stiff

The light, at the same level as her chin, showed the darkness of her wrinkled throat. It deepened the hollows of her high-boned face under a ring of hairpins. To Ethan, still thinking of Mattie, the sight was like the last dream before waking. He felt as if he had never before known what his wife looked like.

She stepped aside without speaking. Mattie and Ethan passed into the kitchen. It had a deadly chill.

"Guess you forgot about us, Zeena," Ethan joked, stamping the snow from his boots.

"No. I just felt so mean I couldn't sleep," Zeena answered.

Mattie came forward. As she untied her wraps, Ethan could see the color of the cherry scarf in her fresh lips and cheeks. "I'm so sorry, Zeena! Isn't there anything I can do to make you feel better?" Mattie asked.

"No, there's nothing." Zeena turned away from her. "You might have shook off that snow outside," she said to her husband.

She walked out of the kitchen ahead of them. She paused in the hall and raised the lamp to light the stairs. The doors of the two bedrooms faced each other across the narrow upper landing. On this night, Ethan couldn't bear the thought that Mattie should see him following Zeena.

"I guess I won't come up yet," he said, turning to go back to the kitchen. "I've got accounts to go over." Zeena stared at him. The flame in the lamp brought out with cruelty the deep lines in her face.

"At this time of night? You'll catch your death. The fire's out long ago," Zeena said.

Without answering, he moved away toward the

kitchen. As he did so, he caught a warning glance from Mattie. Then she began to mount the stairs ahead of Zeena.

"That's so. It *is* powerful cold down here," Ethan agreed. With his head lowered, he went up and followed his wife to their room.

Chapter 3

There was some hauling of lumber to be done at the lower end of the wood lot. Ethan was out early the next day. The winter morning was as clear as crystal. The sunrise burned red in a pure sky. Ethan liked best the stillness of the early morning hours. It was then that he did his clearest thinking.

He and Zeena had not said a word after the door of their room had closed the night before. She had measured out some drops from her medicine bottle and had wrapped her head in a piece of yellow flannel. Then she lay down with her face turned away. Ethan undressed quickly. He blew out the light so he could not see her when he took his place at her side. Not a sound could be heard except Zeena's asthmatic[1] breathing.

Ethan felt confused. There were many things he ought to think about. But at that moment, he could only think of Mattie's touch. He could still feel the warmth of her shoulder against his. Why had he not kissed her when he held her there? A few hours earlier, when they had stood alone outside the house, he would not have dared to think of kissing her. But since he had seen her lips in the lamplight, he felt that they were his.

Now, in the bright morning air, her face was still before him. It was part of the sun's red and of the pure

---

1. **asthmatic** wheezing, coughing, and difficulty in breathing due to asthma

glitter on the snow. How the girl had changed since she had come to Starkfield! He remembered what a small, pale thing she had been the day he met her at the station. All the first winter, she had shivered with cold when the snow beat like hail against the windows. He had been afraid that she would hate the hard life. But she showed no signs of unhappiness. Zeena said that Mattie would have to make the best of Starkfield since she hadn't any other place to go.

Ethan felt sorry for the girl because bad luck had brought her to them. Mattie Silver was the daughter of a cousin of Zeena's, Orin Silver. Orin married a rich girl from Connecticut whose father ran a successful drug business. Orin soon took over the business, and many relatives lent him their savings. But he did not spend his money wisely. To everyone's surprise, he died in debt. The relatives were angry. The shock caused his wife to die soon after. At age twenty, Mattie was left alone to make her way. The only money she had was fifty dollars from the sale of her piano.

Mattie had few skills. She could trim a hat, make molasses candy, recite a few poems, and play the piano. When she had worked for six months on her feet behind the counter of a department store, her health broke down. Her nearest relatives, still angry at Orin, would give her nothing but advice.

When Zeena's doctor told her to find someone to help her around the house, the relatives saw their chance, and they urged Zeena to take the girl. Zeena knew the girl would not be very good at housework, but she knew she could be hard on the girl without risk of losing her.

Zeena's fault-finding was the silent kind. During the first months, Ethan hoped Mattie would stand up to her. But then the situation grew less strained. The pure air and long summer hours in the open gave back life to Mattie. Zeena had more time to think about her many illnesses. She grew less watchful of the girl's mistakes. So, while Ethan struggled on his barren farm, he could at least imagine that peace had come to his house.

Since the previous night, Ethan began to feel a sense of dread. He could not forget Zeena's stubborn silence and Mattie's sudden warning look. His dread was so strong that he tried to think of other things. The hauling would not be over till midday. The lumber was to be delivered to Andrew Hale, the Starkfield builder. It would really be easier for Ethan to send Jotham Powell, the hired man, back to the farm on foot while he drove the load down to the village himself. Just as he was loading the last logs, he saw, once again, the warning look that Mattie had given him the night before.

"If there's going to be any trouble, I want to be there," he thought to himself. Then he told Jotham to unhitch the team and lead them back to the barn.

It was a slow trudge through the heavy fields. When Ethan and Jotham entered the kitchen, Mattie was serving coffee, and Zeena was already at the table. Ethan was shocked at the sight of her. Instead of her usual calico dress and knitted shawl, she wore her best dress of brown wool and a bonnet. On the floor beside her stood his old valise.

"Why, where are you going, Zeena?" he exclaimed.

"I got shooting pains so bad that I'm going over to Bettsbridge to spend the night with Aunt Martha Pierce. I'm going to see that new doctor," she said in a matter-of-fact tone. She might just as well have been saying she was going to the storeroom to get some jam.

Zeena had done such things before. Two or three times, she had suddenly packed Ethan's valise and started off to Bettsbridge or Springfield to get the advice of some new doctor. Ethan had grown to dread these trips because of their cost. Zeena always came back with expensive medicines. Now, he had no doubt that Zeena had spoken the truth the night before when she said she was "too mean" to sleep. All she thought about was her health.

"If you're too busy with the hauling, you can let Jotham Powell drive me over to catch the train at the Flats," she said.

Ethan hardly heard what she was saying. He did some quick thinking. He knew that during the winter months, there was no stage between Starkfield and Bettsbridge. The trains were slow. He realized that Zeena could not be back at the farm before the following evening.

"All I know is," she continued, "I can't go on the way I am much longer. The pains are clear down to my ankles."

"Of course, Jotham will drive you over," Ethan answered. He suddenly realized he was looking at Mattie while Zeena talked to him.

With an effort, he turned his eyes and looked at his wife. She sat opposite the window. The light from the window made her face look unusually pale. He saw the deep, nagging lines on her face. They stretched from her thin nose to the corners of her mouth. Although she was only seven years older than her husband, she looked much older than her age. Ethan was only twenty-eight, and she was already an old woman.

Ethan tried to say something, but there was only one thought on his mind. For the first time since Mattie had come to live with them, Zeena was to be away for a night. He wondered if Mattie was thinking of it, too. He knew that Zeena must be wondering why he did not offer to drive her to the Flats and let Jotham take the lumber to Starkfield. At first, he could not think of a reason for not doing so. Then he said, "I'd take you over myself, only I've got to collect the cash for the lumber."

As soon as he spoke the words, he was sorry. He knew they were untrue. There was no hope of getting an early cash payment from Hale. Worse yet, if Zeena knew he had money, she might buy more medicine. At the moment, his one desire was to avoid the long drive with her.

Zeena made no reply. She did not seem to hear what he said. She pushed her plate aside and took the last sip of her medicine from the bottle.

"It ain't done me a speck of good, but I guess I might as well use it up," she said. Then she pushed the empty bottle toward Mattie. "If you can get the taste out, it will do for pickles."

Chapter 4

As soon as his wife had driven off, Ethan took his coat and cap from the peg. Mattie was washing the dishes, humming a tune from one of the dances from the night before. He said, "So long, Matt." She answered gaily, "So long, Ethan!"

It was warm and bright in the kitchen. The sun slanted through the south window on Mattie's moving figure. Its rays touched the cat dozing in a chair. They glowed on the geraniums that Ethan had planted in the summer to "make a garden" for Mattie. He wanted to stay and watch her tidy up, but he had to get the hauling done and be back at the farm before night.

All the way down to the village, he thought of his return to Mattie. He pictured what it would be like that evening. For the first time, they would be alone together indoors. They would sit there, one on each side of the stove, like a married couple. He would be in his stocking feet, smoking his pipe. She would be laughing and talking in that funny way of hers.

The sweetness of the picture raised his spirits. Ethan, who was usually so silent, whistled and sang aloud as he drove through the snowy fields to the village. He still had a spark of friendliness in him, one that the cold Starkfield winters had not yet put out. Although he had kept to himself in college, he enjoyed it when his friends slapped him on the back and called him "Old Ethe." He missed those times when he returned to Starkfield.

There, the silence deepened around him year after

year. Left alone after his father's accident, he had to carry the burden of the farm and mill. He had no time for fun in the village. When his mother fell ill, the loneliness of the house grew even greater than the loneliness of the fields. His mother was a talker in her day, but after her "trouble," the sound of her voice was rarely heard. During the long winter evenings, Ethan would ask her why she didn't say something. She would just lift a finger and answer, "Because I'm listening."

It was only when his cousin, Zenobia Pierce, came to help nurse his mother that speech was heard in the house again. After the long silence, Zeena's voice was music to Ethan's ears. He felt that he might have "gone like his mother" if the sound of a voice had not come to talk with him. Zeena seemed to understand right away. She told him to "go right along out" and leave her to see to things. Her household skills dazzled him. When his mother died, he was filled with dread. The thought of being left alone on the farm was more than he could bear. Before he knew what he was doing, he had asked her to stay there with him.

When they married, it was agreed that Ethan would sell the farm and sawmill. They both wanted to try their luck in a large town. Ethan loved nature but not farming. He had always wanted to be an engineer and to live in towns where "fellows were doing things." He was eager to see the world. With a "smart" wife like Zeena, he felt he could make a place for himself.

Zeena had come from a village larger than Starkfield. She let Ethan know from the start that life on a lonely farm was not what she expected when she married. Unfortunately, no buyers came to the farm. While he waited, Ethan learned the difficulty of moving Zeena to a new village. She chose to look down on Starkfield, but she could not live in a place that looked down on her. In the larger cities that Ethan liked, she would have been lost. Within a year of their marriage, Zeena developed the "sickliness" that she was known for in their community.

Then she too fell silent. Perhaps it was from life on the farm. Or, perhaps, as she said, it was because Ethan "never listened." This was partly true. When she spoke, it was only to complain. She often complained about things that Ethan couldn't fix. Soon, he formed the habit of not answering her. He began to think of other things when she talked. Of late, her silence began to trouble him. It reminded him of his mother. At times, looking at Zeena's shut face, he felt the chill of fear that she was becoming "strange" like his mother. This troubled Ethan even more. He had felt that way the night before when he had seen her standing in the kitchen doorway.

Now that she had gone to Bettsbridge, he felt at ease. All his thoughts were on spending the evening with Mattie. Only one thing bothered him. He had told Zeena that he would receive cash for the lumber. When Ethan drove into Hale's yard, the builder was just getting out of his sleigh. He greeted Ethan with a friendly, "Hello, Ethe!"

Ethan set about unloading the logs. When he finished, he entered the shed that Hale used as an office. It was warm and friendly, just like the man. Ethan did not know how to begin. He knew Hale's business was good, but his large family often kept him behind in his payments. Finally, Ethan asked for an advance of fifty dollars. The blood rushed to his face when he saw Hale's surprise. It was Hale's custom to pay at the end of three months.

Ethan felt that if he pleaded, Hale might have paid him. But his pride kept him from begging, and he hated lying. If he wanted the money, he wanted it, and it was nobody's business to ask why. He made his request like a man too proud to admit he is stooping. He wasn't much surprised when Hale refused.

"You ain't in a tight place, are you?"

"Not a bit," Ethan's pride replied.

"Well, that's good! Because I *am*. Fact is, I was going to ask you to give me a little extra time. Business isn't good, and I'm fixing up a little house for Ned and Ruth when they're married. I'm glad to do it, but it costs." He looked to Ethan for sympathy. "The young people like things nice. It's not so long ago since you fixed up your own place for Zeena."

Ethan left the grays in Hale's stable and went about some other business in the village. As he walked away, the builder's words lingered in his ears. He reflected grimly that his seven years with Zeena seemed to Starkfield "not so long."

The afternoon was drawing to an end. Ethan had the long street to himself. Suddenly, he heard brisk sleigh bells, and a cutter passed him. Ethan recognized the colt. Denis Eady leaned forward and shouted, "Hello, Ethe!" Then he drove on in the direction of the Frome farm. Ethan's heart almost stopped. What if Denis had heard about Zeena's trip to Bettsbridge? Could he be trying to spend an hour alone with Mattie? Ethan was ashamed of this storm of jealousy.

He walked on to the church corner and entered the shade of the Varnum spruces. This was where he had stood the night before with Mattie. As he approached, he saw two shapes together. Then he heard a kiss and a half-laughing "Oh!" The Varnum gate slammed shut, as one figure ran inside. The other hurried ahead of

Ethan. What did it matter to Ned Hale and Ruth Varnum if they were caught kissing each other? Everyone in Starkfield knew they were engaged. He and Mattie had stood on that very spot with a deep thirst in their hearts for each other. It pained him to think that these two lovers did not have to hide their happiness.

Ethan fetched the grays from the stable and started his long climb back to the farm. He listened for the jingle of sleigh bells, but he heard none. As he drew near to the farm, he saw a light twinkling in the house. "Mattie's up in her room," he said to himself, "fixing herself up for supper." He thought of the night of her arrival. He remembered how Zeena stared at Mattie when she came down to supper with a ribbon around her neck.

He passed by the graves and turned his head to glance at one of the older headstones. It had interested him as a boy because it bore his name.

SACRED TO THE MEMORY
OF
ETHAN FROME AND
ENDURANCE HIS WIFE,
WHO DWELLED
TOGETHER IN PEACE
FOR FIFTY YEARS.

He used to think that fifty years sounded like a long time to live together. He wondered if, when they died, the same words would be written over him and Zeena. He opened the barn door, half fearing to see Denis Eady's colt. But it was not there. Ethan whistled cheerfully as he bedded down the grays. He locked the barn and sprang up the hill to the house. He reached the kitchen door and found it locked. He rattled the handle violently. Then he realized Mattie was alone. It was natural that she lock herself in at nightfall. He called out in a voice that shook with joy, "Hello, Matt!"

The door opened, and Mattie faced him against the black background of the kitchen. She stood just as Zeena had stood, a lifted lamp in her hand. She held the light at the same level. Ethan saw her slim, young throat and her wrist no bigger than a child's. The light touched her shiny lips. Ethan could see the velvet shade of her eyes and the milky whiteness of her fine skin. She wore her usual dress, but she had put a crimson[1] ribbon in her hair. She seemed to Ethan taller, fuller, more womanly in shape and motion.

She stood aside, smiling silently. As Ethan entered, she set the lamp on the table. It was carefully set for supper. He saw fresh doughnuts, stewed blueberries, and his favorite pickles in a dish of red glass. A bright fire glowed in the stove. The cat lay stretched out before it, watching the table with a sleepy eye.

Ethan was overcome with a sense of well-being. He went out into the passage to hang up his coat. When he came back, Mattie had set the teapot on the table. The cat was rubbing itself against her ankles.

"Oh! I nearly tripped over you," she said to the cat.

---

1. **crimson** deep red color

"Well, Matt, any visitors?" Ethan asked as he stooped down to fix the stove.

"Yes, one," she said. He felt a blackness settling on his brows.

"Who was that?" he questioned.

Her eyes danced. "Why, it was Jotham Powell. He came in for a cup of coffee after he got back from the station. The blackness lifted, and light flooded Ethan's brain. "That's all? Well, I hope you gave him some." After a pause, he added, "I suppose he got Zeena over to the Flats all right?"

"Oh, yes, in plenty of time." The name threw a chill between them. Ethan stiffened. They stood looking at each other before Mattie said with a shy laugh, "I guess it's time for supper."

They drew their seats up to the table. "Oh!" said Mattie, as the cat jumped between them into Zeena's empty chair. They laughed again.

Mattie felt his embarrassment. She sipped her tea with downcast eyes. Ethan ate the doughnuts and sweet pickles hungrily. He took a long gulp of tea, cleared his throat, and spoke. "Looks as if there is going to be more snow."

Mattie pretended to be interested. "Is that so? Do you suppose it will make it hard for Zeena getting back?"

Ethan reached over for another helping of pickles. "You never can tell, this time of year. It drifts so bad on the Flats." The mention of the Flats again reminded him of Zeena. He felt as if she were in the room between them.

The cat had crept up on its quiet paws from Zeena's seat to the table. It headed toward the milk jug, which stood between Ethan and Mattie. They both leaned forward at the same moment, and their hands met on the handle of the jug. Mattie's hand was underneath. Ethan kept his hand over Mattie's longer than necessary. The cat tried to leave the table and, in doing so, backed into the pickle dish. It fell to the floor with a crash.

Mattie, in an instant, had sprung from her chair and was down on her knees. "Oh, Ethan! It's all in pieces! What will Zeena say?" By this time, he felt courage. "She'll have to say it to the cat!" he laughed. He knelt down by Mattie's side to scrape up the pickles.

She lifted her fearful eyes to him. "Yes, but you see, she never meant the dish to be used—not even when there was company. I had to get up on the stepladder to get it down from the top shelf of the china closet. She keeps it there with all her best things. Of course, she'll want to know why I did it."

Ethan thought for a moment. "She doesn't have to find out, if you keep quiet. I'll get another just like it tomorrow. I'll go to Shadd's Falls if I have to. Where did it come from?"

"Oh, Ethan, you'll never get another one even there! It was a wedding present. Don't you remember? It came all the way from Philadelphia.

It was from Zeena's aunt. That's why she wouldn't ever use it. Oh Ethan, Ethan, what in the world shall I do?"

She began to cry. He felt as if every one of her tears were pouring over him like burning lead. "Don't Matt, don't, oh, don't!" he begged her. She struggled to her feet, and he rose and followed her. She helplessly spread the broken pieces on the kitchen counter. It seemed to him as if the shattered pieces of their evening lay there.

"Here, give them to me," he said in a commanding voice.

She drew aside, obeying his tone. "Oh, Ethan, what are you going to do?"

Without answering, he picked up the pieces of glass and walked to the china closet in the passage. Reaching his long arm up to the highest shelf, he fit the pieces together perfectly. From below, no one could tell the dish was broken. If he glued it together the next morning, months might pass before his wife would notice what had happened. Meanwhile, he might be able to match the dish at Shadd's Falls. He walked back to the kitchen with a lighter step.

"It's all right, Matt. Come back and finish supper."

Feeling completely secure, she beamed at him through tearful lashes. Ethan's soul swelled with pride, as he saw how his tone had calmed her. She did not even ask what he had done. Except when he was steering a big log down the mountain to his mill, he had never known such a thrilling sense of mastery.[2]

---

2. mastery control, expert skill, or victory

Chapter 5

They finished supper. While Mattie cleared the table, Ethan went outside to look at the cows.

When he returned to the kitchen, Mattie was sewing near the lamp. She had pushed his chair near the stove. The scene was just as he had dreamed. He sat down and drew his pipe from his pocket. He stretched his feet toward the glow. His hard day's work in the cold air made him feel light and lazy as if he were in another world of warmth and peace. There was only one drawback. He couldn't see Mattie. He said, "Come over here and sit by the stove."

Zeena's empty rocking chair stood facing him. Mattie rose obediently. She seated herself in it. For a moment, Ethan could forget Zeena and think only of Mattie. But Mattie felt strange sitting in Zeena's chair. "I can't see to sew," she said and went back to her chair by the lamp.

Ethan got up and pretended to feed the fire in the stove. When he returned to his seat, he pushed it sideways so he could see Mattie's face and the lamplight falling on her hands. The cat, who was watching these unusual movements, jumped into Zeena's chair. It lay there watching them with narrowed eyes. Deep quiet sank into the room. The clock ticked above the dresser. Now and then, a piece of wood fell in the stove. The faint scent of the geraniums mixed with the odor of Ethan's pipe smoke.

Soon, the two began to talk easily and simply. They spoke of everyday things, of the coming of snow and of the next church dance. They even spoke of the loves and quarrels of Starkfield. Ethan began to imagine they had always spent their evenings this way and would always go on doing so. . . .

"This is the night we were to have gone coasting, Matt." He said it as if they had all the time in the world and could go on any night they chose.

She smiled back at him. "I guess you forgot!"

"No, I didn't forget. But it's too dark outdoors tonight. We might go tomorrow if there's a moon."

She laughed. "That would be lovely, Ethan!"

He kept his eyes fixed on her. He marveled at the way her face changed as they talked, like a wheat field under a summer breeze.

"Would you be scared to go down the Corbury road with me on a night like this?" he asked.

Her cheeks burned redder. "I ain't any more scared than you are!"

"Well, *I'd* be scared then. I wouldn't do it. That's an ugly corner down by the big elm. If a fellow didn't keep his eyes open, he'd go right into that elm tree." He enjoyed the feeling that he was protecting her. He added, "I guess we're well enough here."

She let her eyelids sink slowly in the way he loved. "Yes, we're well enough here," she sighed.

Her tone was so sweet that he took the pipe from his mouth and drew his chair to the table. Leaning forward, he touched the far end of the strip of brown cloth she was hemming. "Say Matt," he began with a smile, "what do you think I saw under the Varnum spruces coming along home tonight? I saw a friend of yours getting kissed."

He wanted to speak the words all evening. But now that he had spoken them, they seemed out of place. Mattie blushed to the roots of her hair. She pulled her needle quickly through the cloth. "I suppose it was Ruth and Ned," she said in a low voice.

Suddenly, he knew he had touched on something. Her flushed face told him something about her. He knew that most young men made nothing at all of giving a pretty girl a kiss. Then he remembered the night before. When he put his arm around Mattie, she had not stopped him. But that had been outside. Now in the warm room under the light of the lamp, she seemed hard to get near.

"I suppose they'll be setting the date before long," he said to ease the strain of the moment.

"Yes, I wouldn't be surprised if they get married sometime in the summer." She said the word *married* as if her voice kissed it. A pang shot through Ethan. Twisting away from her in his chair, he said, "It'll be your turn next, I guess."

She laughed a little uncertainly. "Why do you keep on saying that?"

"I guess I do it to get used to the idea."

He moved to the table again. She sewed on in silence with her eyes down. After some time, she said without lifting her head, "It's not because you think Zeena's got anything against me, is it?"

The dread he felt the night before started to rise up in him. "Why, what do you mean?" he stammered.

She raised fearful eyes to him. Her work dropped on the table between them. "I don't know. I thought last night she was upset with me."

"I'd like to know about what," he growled.

"Nobody can tell with Zeena." It was the first time they had ever spoken so openly about Zeena's attitude toward Mattie. "She hasn't said anything to *you* has she?" Mattie continued.

He shook his head. "No, not a word."

She tossed her hair back from her forehead with a laugh. "I guess I'm just nervous, then. I'm not going to think about it anymore."

"Oh, no—let's not think about it, Matt!"

The sudden heat of his tone brought the color back to Mattie's face. She sat silent, her hands on her sewing. It seemed to Ethan that a warm current flowed toward him along the strip of the cloth that lay between them. Cautiously, he slid his hand, palm down, along the table till his finger tips touched the end of the cloth. A faint movement of her lashes seemed to show that she was aware of his gesture. She let her hands lie still on the other end of the strip of cloth. They sat like that for a while. Then Ethan heard a sound behind him and turned his head. The cat jumped from Zeena's chair and darted after a mouse. The sudden movement left the empty chair rocking. It seemed almost ghost-like in appearance.

"She'll be rocking in it herself this time tomorrow," Ethan thought. "I've been in a dream. This is the only evening we'll ever have together."

The return to reality was painful. Mattie felt his mood change. She looked up at him with great effort. Her glance fell on his hand. Now it completely covered the end of her sewing. It was as if it were a part of herself. He saw a slight tremble of her face. Without knowing what he did, he stooped his head and kissed the bit of cloth in his grasp. As his lips rested on it, he felt it glide slowly from beneath them. He saw that Mattie had risen and was silently rolling up her sewing. She tied it with a pin. Then she took her thimble and scissors and placed her work in the box. He stood up also and looked around the room. The clock above the dresser struck eleven.

"Is the fire all right?" she asked in a low voice.

He opened the door of the stove and poked the wood embers. When he raised himself again, he saw that she was dragging the cat's bed toward the stove. When these nightly chores were over, there was nothing left to do. Ethan brought in the tin candlestick from the passage, lit the candle, and then blew out the lamp. He put the candlestick in Mattie's hand. She went out of the kitchen ahead of him. The light that she carried made her dark hair look like a drift of mist on the moon.

"Good night, Matt," he said as she put her foot on the first step of the stairs.

She turned and looked at him a moment. "Good night, Ethan," she answered and went up.

When the door of her room had closed, he remembered that he had not even touched her hand.

Chapter 6

The next morning at breakfast, Jotham Powell sat between them. Ethan tried to hide his joy by throwing scraps to the cat and complaining about the weather. He didn't even offer to help Mattie when she cleared the dishes. He didn't know why he was so happy. Nothing had changed in his life or hers. He had not even touched the tip of her fingers or looked her full in the eyes. But their evening together had given him a vision of what life at her side might be like. He was glad now that he had done nothing to trouble the sweetness of the picture. He had an idea that she knew what had stopped him.

There was a load of lumber to be hauled to the village. Jotham Powell did not work regularly for Ethan in the winter. But he had "come around" to help with the job. A wet snow, melting to sleet, had fallen in the night. It had turned the roads to glass. Both men agreed that the weather would get mild by the afternoon. It would be safer to travel then. Ethan suggested they load up the lumber at the woodlot as they had done the morning before. They would go to Starkfield later in the day. Ethan would send Jotham to the Flats to get Zeena while he took the lumber down to the village himself. He told Jotham to go out and harness up the grays for hauling.

For a moment, he and Mattie had the kitchen to themselves. She was washing the breakfast dishes. Her slim arms were bare to the elbow in the steaming, hot water. Ethan stood looking at her, his heart in his throat. He wanted to say, "We shall never be alone again like this." Instead, he reached for his tobacco pouch on the shelf. Putting it in his pocket, he said, "I guess I can make it home for dinner."

She answered, "All right, Ethan." He heard her singing over the dishes as he went.

As soon as the lumber was loaded, he meant to send Jotham back to the farm. Then he would hurry on foot to the village to buy glue for the pickle dish. With ordinary luck, he should have had time to carry out his plan. But everything went wrong from the start. On the way over to the woodlot, one of the grays slipped on some ice and cut his knee. Then, a sleety rain began. The lumber was slippery. It took twice as long to load the sledge.[1] He had to give up going to the village because he wanted to lead the injured horse home and wash the cut himself.

Ethan hoped to start out with the lumber as soon as he finished his midday meal. He might then get back to the farm with the glue before Jotham had time to fetch Zeena from the Flats. But he knew the chance was a slight one. It turned on the state of the roads and the possible lateness of Zeena's train. As soon as his meal was over, he gave Mattie a quick look. Then he said under his breath, "I'll be back early."

He had driven his load halfway to the village when Jotham Powell passed him going to the Flats. "I'll have to hurry up to get back in time for Mattie," he thought to himself.

When he got to the village, he worked like ten men unloading the lumber. Then he quickly went over to Michael Eady's for the glue to repair the pickle dish. Eady and his helper were gone. Young Denis was sit-

---

1. **sledge** a sled for carrying loads over ice or snow

ting by the stove with a group of other young men. They greeted Ethan, but no one knew where to find the glue. As Denis searched, Ethan longed for his last moments with Mattie.

"Looks as if we're all sold out. But if you wait around till the old man comes back, maybe he can find it," Denis said.

"Thanks, but I'll try to get it down at Mrs. Homan's," Ethan answered, burning to be gone.

Ethan climbed to the sledge and drove on to the other store. Widow Homan wanted to know what the glue was for. She asked whether common paste would work if she couldn't find the glue. Finally, she found the last bottle hiding among cough drops. "I hope Zeena ain't broken anything she likes," she called after him as he turned the grays toward home.

The sleet had changed to a steady rain. The horses had heavy work even without a load behind them. Once or twice, hearing sleigh bells, Ethan turned his head. He imagined that Zeena and Jotham might pass him and get back to the farm before he did. But luckily, they were not in sight.

The barn was empty when the horses turned into it. He barely tended them. Then he hurried up to the house and pushed open the kitchen door.

Mattie was there alone, as he had pictured her. She was bending over a pan on the stove. At the sound of his steps, she turned with a start and sprang to him.

"See, here, Matt, I've got the glue to mend the dish with! Let me get at it quick," he cried waving the bottle in his hand. He put her aside gently with his hand, but she did not seem to hear him.

"Oh, Ethan—Zeena's come," she said in a whisper. She clutched his sleeve. They stood and stared at each other, pale with guilt.

"But the sleigh's not in the barn!" Ethan stammered.

"Jotham Powell brought some goods over from the Flats for his wife. He didn't stay. He drove right on home with them," she explained.

He gazed blankly about the cold kitchen. It looked ugly in the rainy winter light. "How is she?" he asked, dropping his voice to Mattie's whisper.

She looked away from him uncertainly. "I don't know. She went right up to her room."

"She didn't say anything?"

"No."

Ethan put the bottle back in his pocket. "Don't worry. I'll come down and mend it in the night," he said. He put on his coat again and went into the barn to feed the grays. When he entered the kitchen again, the lamp was lit. He saw the same scene he had seen the night before. The table had been carefully set, a clear fire glowed in the stove, and the cat dozed in its warmth. Mattie came forward carrying a plate of doughnuts.

She and Ethan looked at each other in silence. Then she said, as she had said the night before, "I guess it's about time for supper."

Chapter 7

Ethan went out into the passage to hang up his wet clothes. He listened for Zeena's step. Not hearing it, he called her name up the stairs. She did not answer. He waited a moment. Then he went up and opened her door. The room was almost dark. He could see her stiff outline against the window pane. She had not taken off her traveling dress.

"Well, Zeena," he said from the doorway, "supper's about ready. Ain't you coming?"

She remained seated. "I don't feel as if I could touch a bite."

He could think of nothing more to say. So he tried, "You must be tired after the long ride."

Turning her head at this, she answered gravely, "I'm a great deal sicker than you think."

Her words fell on his ear with a strange shock. He had often heard her say them before. What if at last they were true?

He stepped into the dim room. "I hope that's not so, Zeena," he said.

She continued to gaze at him. "I've got complications." She said this as if she were singled out for a great fate.

Ethan knew that the word was serious. Almost everybody in the neighborhood had "troubles," but only the chosen few had "complications." People struggled on for years with "troubles," but they almost always died from "complications."

"Is that what the new doctor told you?" he asked, lowering his voice.

"Yes. He says any regular doctor would want me to have an operation."

Zeena had always thought that operations were improper for women. Ethan had been glad of this because of the large cost. Now, he wondered, "What do you know about this doctor anyway? Nobody ever told you that before."

"I didn't need to have anybody tell me I was losing ground every day. Everybody but you could see it. And everybody in Bettsbridge knows about Dr. Buck. He helped Eliza Spears when she was wasting away with kidney trouble. Now she's up and around, singing in the choir," she replied.

"Well, I'm glad of that. You must do just what he tells you," Ethan said with sympathy.

She was still looking at him. "I mean to," she said. He was struck by a new note in her voice. It was neither whining nor angry, but clearly firm.

"What does he want you to do?" he asked. Visions of new costs came to his mind.

"He wants me to have a hired girl. He says I shouldn't have to do a single thing around the house."

"A hired girl?" Ethan stood stunned.

"Yes. And Aunt Martha found me one right off. Everybody said I was lucky to get a girl to come way out here. I agreed to give her a dollar extra to make sure. She'll be over tomorrow afternoon."

Ethan felt a wave of anger and sorrow. He knew she would demand money, but he was not ready for such an expense. He no longer believed Zeena was so sick. He thought that her trip was a scheme to make him pay for a servant.

"If you meant to hire a girl, you ought to have told me before you started," he said.

"How did I know what Dr. Buck was going to say?"

"Oh, Dr. Buck," Ethan laughed. "Did Dr. Buck tell you how I was going to pay her wages?"

Her voice rose furiously with his. "No, he didn't. I was ashamed to tell *him* that you wouldn't give me the money to get back my health. Especially when I lost it nursing your own mother!"

"*You* lost your health nursing mother?"

"Yes, and my folks all told me at the time you couldn't do no less than marry me after—"

"Zeena!"

In the darkness, their thoughts seemed to dart at each other like snakes shooting poison. Ethan felt the horror of the scene. He was ashamed of his own part in it. It was as senseless and cruel as a physical fight between two enemies. Ethan looked for matches on the shelf and lit one candle in the room. Zeena's face stood out grimly against the window pane. It was the first scene of open anger between the couple in their sad seven years together. Ethan felt as if he had lost the upper hand, but the problem had to be dealt with.

"You know I haven't got the money to pay for a girl, Zeena. You'll have to send her back. I can't do it."

"The doctor says it'll be my death if I go on slaving the way I've had to."

"Slaving!" He stopped himself again. "You won't have to lift a hand, if the doctor says so. I'll do everything 'round the house myself."

She broke in. "You don't spend time enough on the farm already." This was true, and Ethan could think of no other answer. "Better send me over to the poor house and be done with it. I guess there's been Fromes there before now."

The tease burned into him, but he let it pass. "I haven't got the money. That settles it."

There was a moment's pause in the struggle. Then Zeena said in a firm voice, "I thought you were to get fifty dollars from Andrew Hale for the lumber."

"Andrew Hale never pays under three months." He had hardly spoken when he remembered the excuse he had made for not driving her to the station.

"Why, you told me yesterday you'd fixed it up with him to pay cash down. That's why you couldn't drive me to the Flats."

Ethan was not good at deceiving[1] people. He had never before been caught in a lie. He could think of no answer. "I guess that was a mix-up," he stammered.

"You ain't got the money."

"No."

"And you ain't going to get it?"

"No."

"Well, I couldn't know that when I hired the girl, could I?"

"No." He paused to control his voice. "But you know it now. You're a poor man's wife, Zeena. I'll do the best I can for you." He started going down to supper. "There's a whole lot more I can do for you, and Mattie—"

Zeena stopped him. "At least, we won't have the cost of Mattie's board[2] anymore."

The mention of Mattie made Ethan stop short. He turned around and closed the door. "Mattie's board?"

---

1. **deceiving** misleading; using trickery
2. **board** expenses for food and lodging

Zeena laughed. "You didn't suppose I was going to keep two girls, did you? No wonder you were scared at the cost!"

He was still confused. "I don't know what you mean," he said. "Mattie Silver's not a hired girl. She's your relation."

"She's a pauper[3] that's hung onto us all after her father had done his best to ruin us. I've kept her here a whole year. It's somebody else's turn now."

As the sharp words shot out, Ethan heard a tap on the door.

"Ethan! Zeena!" Mattie's voice sounded gaily from the landing. "Do you know what time it is? Supper's been ready half an hour."

"I'm not coming down to supper," Zeena called out from her seat. Ethan opened the door. "Go along, Matt. Zeena's just a little tired. I'm coming."

He heard her say "All right!" Then he shut the door and turned back to his wife. Her mood was unchanged, and her face was set. He was overcome with a sense of despair and helplessness.

"You ain't going to do it, Zeena?"

"Do what?" she asked between flattened lips.

"Send Mattie away, like this?"

"I never bargained to take her for life!"

He continued with rising anger. "You can't put her out of the house like a thief. She's a poor girl without friends or money. She's done her best for you, and she's got no place to go to. You may forget she's your kin, but everybody else will remember it. If you do a thing like that, what do you suppose folks will say of you?"

Zeena waited for a moment, as if to show the

---

3. **pauper** a very poor person

contrast between his anger and her calm. Then she answered in the same smooth voice. "I know well enough what they say about my having kept her here as long as I have."

Ethan's hand dropped from the doorknob. He had been holding it tightly since Mattie had gone downstairs. His wife's answer was like a knife across his muscles. He felt weak and powerless. He had meant to humble[4] himself. He wanted to argue that it didn't cost much to keep Mattie. After all, he could fix up a place in the attic for the hired girl. But listening to Zeena's words, he knew such pleading was dangerous.

"You mean to tell her she's got to go at once?"

As if trying to make him see reason, Zeena replied with fairness. "The girl will be over from Bettsbridge tomorrow, and she's got to have somewhere to sleep."

Ethan looked at Zeena with loathing.[5] She seemed like an evil force. She had mastered him, and he hated her. Mattie was her relation, not his. There was no way he could force Zeena to keep the girl under her roof. All the long sadness of his past, of his hardships and failed youth, rose up in his soul.

He turned his anger toward the woman who at every step had barred his way. She had taken everything else from him. Now she meant to take the one thing that made up for all the others. For a moment, such a flame of hate rose in him that it ran down his arm. Taking a wild step forward, he clenched his fist against her. Then he stopped.

"You're . . . you're not coming down?" he said in a confused voice.

---

4. **humble** to act in a respectful, modest way
5. **loathing** hatred, disgust

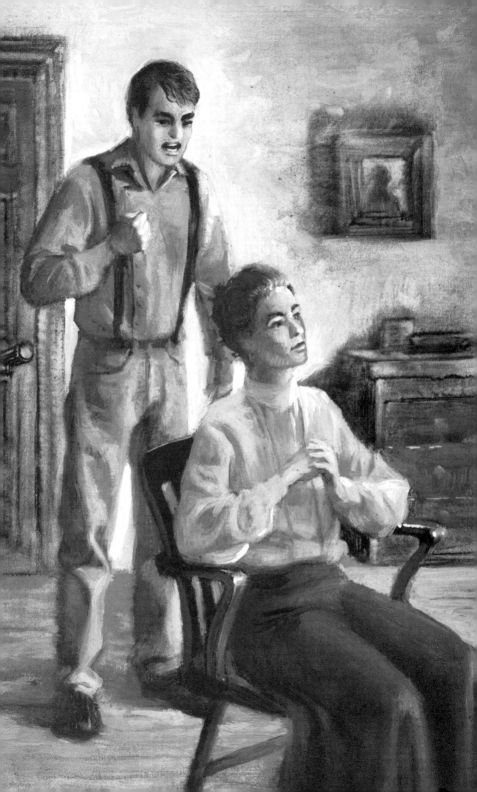

"No. I guess I'll lay down on the bed a little while," she answered mildly. He turned and walked out of the room.

In the kitchen, Mattie was sitting by the stove. The cat was curled up on her knees. Mattie sprang to her feet as Ethan entered. Then she carried the covered dish of meat pie to the table.

"I hope Zeena isn't sick?" she asked.

"No."

Her eyes shone at him across the table. "Well, sit right down then. You must be starving." She uncovered the pie. So they were to have one more evening together, her happy eyes seemed to say!

Ethan couldn't eat. Disgust took him by the throat, and he laid down his fork. Mattie watched him tenderly. "Why Ethan, what's the matter? Don't it taste right?"

"Yes, it's first rate. Only I—" He pushed his plate away and walked around the table to her side. She turned to him with frightened eyes.

"Ethan, there's something wrong! I *knew* there was!"

She seemed to melt against him in terror. He caught her in his arms and held her fast. He could feel her eyelashes beating against his cheek like butterflies caught in a net.

"What is it? What is it?" she stammered. But Ethan had found her lips at last. At the moment, he was only aware of the joy they gave him.

She waited, caught in the same strong feelings. Then she drew back, pale and troubled. He cried out, as if he saw her drowning in a dream. "You can't go, Matt! I'll never let you!"

"Go? Go?" she stammered. "Must I go?"

Ethan was overcome with shame. He felt cruel for telling her the news so suddenly. His head spun, and he had to support himself against the table. All the while, he felt as if he were still kissing her and yet dying of thirst for her lips.

"Ethan, what has happened? Is Zeena mad at me?"

"No, no," he comforted her. "It's not that. But this new doctor has scared her about herself. You know she believes all that they say the first time she sees them. And this one's told her she won't get well unless she stays in bed and doesn't do a thing about the house—not for months."

He paused. His eyes wandered sadly. She stood silent a moment, drooping before him like a broken branch. She was so small and weak-looking that it broke his heart. But suddenly, she lifted her head and looked straight at him.

"And she wants somebody handier in my place? Is that it?"

"That's what she says tonight."

"If she says it tonight, she'll say it tomorrow."

They both knew the truth. Zeena never changed her mind. There was a long silence between them. Then Mattie said in a low voice, "Don't be sorry, Ethan."

"Oh, God—oh, God," he groaned. The glow of passion he felt for her melted into an aching tenderness. He saw her quick eyelids beating back the tears. He longed to take her in his arms and soothe her.

"You're letting your supper get cold," she said.

"Oh, Matt, where will you go?"

Her lids sank, and she began to tremble. He saw that, for the first time, she thought of the future. "I might get something to do over at Stamford." Her voice broke, as if knowing that he knew she had no hope.

He dropped back into his seat and hid his face in his hands. He felt helpless at the thought of Mattie's setting out alone to look for work. What chance did she have among the millions seeking work? She was untrained and had no experience. He sprang up suddenly.

"You can't go Matt! I won't let you. She's always had her way, but I mean to have mine now!"

Mattie lifted her hand with a quick warning. He heard his wife's steps behind him. Zeena came into the room, dragging her heels with each step. She quietly took her seat between them.

"I feel a little better. Dr. Buck says I ought to eat all I can," she said in her flat whine. She reached across the table for the teapot. Her good dress had been replaced by the black calico-and-brown knitted shawl she wore every day. She poured out her tea, helping herself to pie and pickles. Before she began to eat, she fixed her false teeth. The cat rubbed itself against her ankles.

Ethan sat speechless. Mattie nibbled bravely at her food and asked Zeena questions about her trip. When supper was over, Zeena rose from her seat and pressed her hand over her heart. "That pie of yours is always a little heavy, Matt," she said.

"I've a good mind to go and hunt up those stomach powders I got last year," she continued. "I ain't tried them for awhile. Maybe they'll help the heartburn."

Mattie lifted her eyes. "Can't I get them for you, Zeena?" she asked.

"No. They're in a place you don't know about." Zeena replied with one of her dark, secret looks.

Zeena went out of the kitchen. Mattie rose and began to clear the dishes. As she passed Ethan's chair, their eyes met and clung together sadly. The warm kitchen looked as peaceful as the night before. The cat sprang to Zeena's rocking chair. The heat of the fire was beginning to draw out the scent of the geraniums. Ethan dragged himself to his feet.

"I'll go out and take a look around," he said, going toward the passage to get his lantern.

As he reached the door, he met Zeena coming back into the room. Her lips were tight with anger. The shawl had slipped from her shoulders and was dragging at her heels. In her hands she carried the broken pieces of the red glass pickle dish.

"I'd like to know who done this," she said, looking sternly from Ethan to Mattie.

There was no answer. She continued in a trembling voice. "I went to get those powders I'd put away in father's eyeglass case on top of the china closet. I put all my things there so folks can't meddle with them." Her voice broke, and two small tears hung on her lashes and ran down her cheeks. "It takes a stepladder to get to the top shelf. I put Aunt Maple's pickle dish up there on purpose when we was married. It's never been down since, except for the spring cleaning. And then I always lifted it with my own hands so it wouldn't get broke."

She laid the pieces tenderly on the table. "I want to know who done this."

Ethan turned back into the room and faced her. "I can tell you then. The cat done it."

"The *cat* ?"

"That's what I said."

She looked at him hard. Then she turned her eyes to Mattie, who was carrying the dishpan to the table.

"I'd like to know how the cat got into my china closet," she said.

"Chasing mice, I guess," Ethan answered. "There was a mouse running around the kitchen all last evening."

"I knew the cat was a smart cat," she said in a high voice. "But I didn't know he was smart enough to pick up the pieces of my pickle dish and lay them together, edge by edge. And on the very shelf he knocked them off of!"

Mattie suddenly drew her arms out of the steaming water. "It wasn't Ethan's fault, Zeena! The cat *did* break the dish. But I got it down from the china closet. I'm the one to blame for its getting broken."

Zeena stood beside her ruined treasure. She stiffened into a stony picture of anger. "*You* got down my pickle dish! What for?"

A bright flush flew to Mattie's cheeks. "I wanted to make the supper table pretty," she said.

"You wanted to make the supper table pretty. And you waited till my back was turned. And then you took the thing I love the most of everything I've got, and wouldn't ever use, not even when the minister comes to dinner or Aunt Martha Pierce from Bettsbridge—" Zeena paused with a gasp.

"You're a bad girl, Mattie Silver. And I always known it. It's the way your father begun. I was warned of it when I took you. I tried to keep my things where you couldn't get at them. Now you've taken from me the one thing I cared for most of all!" She broke off in a short sob. When it passed, it left her more than ever like a shape of stone.

"If I had listened to folks, you would have gone before now. This wouldn't have happened," she said. Gathering up the bits of broken glass, she went out of the room as if she carried a dead body.

Chapter 8

Before she had died, his mother had given him the room behind the "best parlor." He had nailed up shelves for his books and built himself a sofa out of boards and a mattress. He had tried to make it look like the study of a kind minister he knew who had lent him some books. He still escaped there in the summer. But when Mattie came to live at the farm, he had given her his stove. Since then, he wasn't able to use the room for most of the winter.

To this room he escaped as soon as the house was quiet. After Zeena left the kitchen, he and Mattie had stood speechless. Neither approached the other. Then Mattie returned to her task of cleaning up the kitchen. Ethan took his lantern and went on his usual rounds outside the house. The kitchen was empty when he came back. His tobacco pouch and pipe had been laid on the table. Under them was a scrap of paper. On the paper, three words were written: "Don't trouble, Ethan."

Going into his cold, dark study, he placed the lantern on the table. Placing the message under the light, he read it again and again. It was the first time Mattie had ever written to him. It made him feel near her. It also deepened his sadness. It reminded him that soon they would have no other way of being together. What he would do for the life of her smile and the warmth of her voice! For now, all he had was cold paper and dead words.

Feelings of rebellion[1] stormed in him. He was too young, too strong, too full of life to see all his hopes destroyed. Must he wear out all his years at the side of a bitter, complaining woman? She was a hundred times more bitter than when he had married her. It seemed to Ethan that the only pleasure left to her was to cause him pain.

He wrapped himself in his old raccoon coat and lay down on the sofa to think. He knew of a man over the mountain who had escaped from just such a sad life. He was a young fellow about Ethan's age. He went west with the girl he cared for. His wife divorced him. He married the girl and became rich. Ethan had seen the couple the summer before at Shadd's Falls. The wife he left had not done badly either. Her husband had given her the farm. She managed to sell it. With the money, she started a lunchroom at Bettsbridge.

Ethan was excited by the thought. Why shouldn't he leave with Mattie the next day, instead of letting her go alone? He could hide his bags under the seat of the sleigh. Zeena would think nothing till she went upstairs for her nap and found a letter on the bed.

He sprung to his feet, lit the lantern, and sat down at the table. He began to write. "Zeena, I've done all I could for you, and I don't see as it's been any use. I don't blame you, nor do I blame myself. Maybe both of us will do better separate. I'm going to try my luck West. You can sell the farm and mill and keep the money."

His pen stopped on the word *money*. If he gave he farm and mill to Zeena, what would be left for him to start his new life? Once in the West, he was sure of getting work. He didn't fear trying his chances

---

1. **rebellion** opposition to authority or control; fighting back

alone. But with Mattie depending on him, the case was different.

What about Zeena? The farm and mill were in debt. Even if she found a buyer, she would barely clear a thousand dollars on the sale. Meanwhile, how could she keep the farm going? She could go back to her people and see what they could do for her. It was just the fate she was forcing on Mattie. Why not let her try it herself? Maybe by the time she found out where he was and divorced him, he would have enough money to pay her support.

As he took up his pen, his eye fell on an old copy of the *Bettsbridge Eagle*. On the open page, he saw an advertisement: "Trips to the West: Reduced Rates." The paper fell from his hand. Ethan pushed aside the unfinished letter. A moment ago, he had been wondering what he and Mattie would live on in the West. Now he saw that he didn't even have the money to take her there.

He knew he could not borrow any money. Six months ago, he had given his only security to repair the mill. He knew that without security, no one in Starkfield would lend him ten dollars. There was no way out, none. He was a prisoner for life, and now his one hope was gone.

He crept back to the sofa, stretching out his weary legs. He felt as if they would never move again. Tears rose in his throat and slowly burned their way to his lids. As he lay there, he watched the glow of the moon through the window pane. This was the night he was to have taken Mattie coasting. The moonlight was there to guide them! He looked out at the slopes bathed in light. The dark woods were edged in silver, and the hills seemed purple against the sky. The beauty of the night seemed to increase his suffering.

He fell asleep, and when he woke, he saw the dawn of a red sun. He said to himself, "This is Matt's last day." He tried to think of what life would be like without her. As he stood there, he heard a step behind him as she entered the room.

"Oh, Ethan, were you here all night?"

She looked so small in her poor dress with the red scarf tied about her. "You must be frozen," she continued.

He drew nearer. "How did you know I was here."

"Because I heard you after I went to bed. I listened all night. And you didn't come up."

All his tender feelings rushed to his lips. He looked at her and said, "I'll come right along and make the kitchen fire."

They went back to the kitchen. He fetched the coal for the fire. She brought in the milk and the cold meat pie. Warmth began to come from the stove. Ethan's dark thoughts melted as he watched Mattie go about her work just as she had done each and every morning. How was it possible that she would no longer be part of this scene?

He went up to Mattie as she bent over the stove. He laid his hand on her arm. "I don't want you to trouble, either," he said with a smile.

She blushed and whispered back. "No, Ethan, I ain't going to trouble."

"I guess things will straighten out," he added.

There was no answer but a quick blink of her eyelids. He went on. "She ain't said anything this morning?"

"No. I haven't seen her yet."

"Don't you take any notice when you do."

With that warning, he left her and went out to the cow barn. Jotham Powell was walking up the hill. He rested his pitchfork to say, "Daniel Byrne's going over to the Flats today at noon. He can take Mattie's trunk along. That will make it easier riding when I take her over in the sleigh."

Ethan looked at him blankly. Jotham continued, "Mrs. Frome said the new girl will be at the Flats at five. I was to take Mattie then so she could catch the six o'clock train for Stamford."

Ethan felt the blood rushing to his temples. He had to wait a moment before he could say, "Oh, I ain't so sure about Mattie's going."

"That so?" said Jotham, and they went on with their work.

When they returned to the kitchen, the two women were already at breakfast. Zeena was full of energy. She drank two cups of coffee and fed the cat. Next, she went over to the window and snipped two leaves from the geraniums. Then she turned to Jotham and asked, "What time did you say Daniel Byrne would be along?"

The hired man glanced at Ethan. "'Round about noon," he said.

Zeena turned to Mattie. "That trunk of yours is too heavy for the sleigh. Daniel Byrne will be 'round to take it over to the Flats," she said.

"I'm thankful to you, Zeena," said Mattie.

"I'd like to go over things with you first," Zeena continued. "I know there's a towel missing. And I can't make out what you've done with that match case that used to be in the parlor."

She went out, followed by Mattie. When the men were alone, Jotham said to Ethan, "I guess I better let Daniel come 'round, then."

Ethan finished his usual morning tasks in the house and barn. Then he said to Jotham, "I'm going down to Starkfield. Tell them not to wait for me for dinner."

The feeling of rebellion had broken out in him again. What seemed impossible in the light of day had happened. How could he help send Mattie away? He no longer felt like a man. What must Mattie think of him? As he rode along to the village, he struggled with these confused thoughts. He made up his mind to do something, but he did not know what it would be.

The early mist had gone, and the fields lay like silver under the sun. It was one of those days when the glow of winter shines through a pale haze of spring. Every part of the road was alive with the thought of Mattie. There was hardly a tree branch against the sky that did not remind him of her. The sound of the bird in the ash tree was so like her laughter that his heart grew full. All these things made him see that something must be done at once.

Suddenly, he got an idea. He knew Andrew Hale was a kind man. What if he told him that Zeena was in ill health, and that they had to hire a servant? Perhaps Hale would change his mind and give him a small advance on the lumber.

The more he thought of the plan, the more hopeful it seemed. What did his pride matter as long as he could have Mattie? If he could get Mr. Hale's help, he felt certain of success. With fifty dollars in his pocket, nothing could keep him from Mattie.

He knew he had to reach Starkfield before Hale started for his work. Hale had a job down the Corbury road. Ethan knew Hale would leave early. He walked quickly. As he reached the foot of the hill, he saw Hale's sleigh in the distance. He hurried to meet it, but as it got closer, he could see it was driven by the builder's youngest boy. The person at his side was Mrs.

Hale herself. Ethan waved for them to stop. Mrs. Hale leaned forward, her pink, wrinkled skin shining with kindness.

"Mr. Hale? Why, yes, you will find him down home now. He ain't going to work before noon. He woke up with a touch of lumbago[2] this morning. I made him put on one of Dr. Kidder's plasters and told him to sit by the fire."

She looked so kind to Ethan, just like a mother. She bent over to add, "I only just heard about Zeena. I'm real sorry she's feeling so bad again! I hope the new doctor thinks he can do something for her. I don't know anybody 'round here that's had more sickness than Zeena. I always tell Mr. Hale, I don't know what she would have done if she hadn't had you to look after her. I used to say the same thing about your mother. You've had an awful mean time, Ethan Frome."

Before she drove off, she gave him a last nod of sympathy. Ethan stood in the middle of the road and stared at the sleigh.

It was a long time since anyone had spoken to him so kindly as Mrs. Hale. Most people didn't care about his troubles. But Mrs. Hale said, "You've had an awful mean time, Ethan Frome." It made him feel less alone with his suffering. If the Hales felt sorry for him, they would surely lend him the money.

He started down the road toward their house. But after walking a few yards, he stopped. The blood rushed to his face. For the first time, he saw what he was about to do. Mrs. Hale's words made him see it. He was planning to take advantage of the Hales' sympathy. He was about to get money from them on a lie.

---

2. lumbago a painful muscle ache, especially in the lower part of the back

Suddenly, he saw how far madness had carried him. As he saw it, the madness fell away. He understood his life as it was. He was a poor man and the husband of a sickly woman. If he left her, she would be alone without any means to take care of herself. He could only leave her by tricking two kind people who felt sorry for him.

He turned and walked slowly back to the farm.

Chapter 9

Outside the kitchen door, Daniel Byrne sat in his sleigh behind a big-boned gray. Ethan went into the kitchen and found his wife by the stove. Her head was wrapped in her shawl. She was reading a book on *Kidney Troubles and Their Cure*. He had paid for the book only a few days before.

Zeena did not move or look up when he entered. After a moment, he asked, "Where's Mattie?"

Without lifting her eyes from the page, she replied, "I guess she's getting down her trunk."

The blood rushed to his face. "Getting down her trunk—alone?"

"Jotham Powell's down in the woodlot, and Daniel Byrne says he can't leave that horse."

Without hearing the end of her words, Ethan sprang up the stairs. The door of Mattie's room was shut. He waited a moment on the landing. "Matt," he said in a low voice. There was no answer. He put his hand on the doorknob.

He had never been in her room before except once in early summer. He had gone there to plaster a leak in the roof. He remembered exactly how everything looked. She had a red-and-white quilt on her narrow bed. There was a pretty pin cushion on her chest of drawers. A photograph of her mother was in a frame on the wall. Now, all her things were gone. The room looked as bare and cold as on the day she had come to live with them.

In the middle of the floor stood Mattie's trunk. She was sitting on it in her Sunday best. Her back was turned to the door, and her face was in her hands. She had not heard Ethan's call because she was sobbing. She had not even heard his step till he stood close behind her and laid his hands on her shoulders.

"Matt—oh, don't—oh, *Matt!*"

She started up, lifting her wet face to his. "Ethan, I thought I wasn't ever going to see you again!"

He took her in his arms, pressing her close. With a trembling hand, he smoothed away the hair from her forehead.

"Not see me again? What do you mean?"

She sobbed out, "Jotham said you told him we wasn't to wait for you for dinner. I thought—"

"You thought I meant not to come?" He finished the words for her grimly.

She clung to him without answering. He laid his lips on her hair. It was soft like certain mosses on warm hills. To him, it had the faint odor of fresh sawdust in the sun.

Through the door, they heard Zeena's voice calling from below. "Daniel Byrne says you better hurry up if you want him to take that trunk."

They drew apart with fearful faces. Fighting words rushed to Ethan's lips, but they made no sound. Mattie found her handkerchief and dried her eyes. Then she bent down and took hold of a handle of her trunk.

Ethan put her aside. "You let go, Matt," he ordered her.

She answered. "It takes two to get it 'round the corner." Together, they took the trunk to the landing.

"Now let go," he repeated. Then he carried the trunk down on his shoulders. He put it in the passage to the kitchen. Zeena was sitting by the stove. She did not lift her head from her book as he passed. Mattie followed him out the door and helped him lift the trunk into the back of the sleigh.

It seemed to Ethan that his heart was bound with cords. Twice he opened his lips to speak to Mattie and found no breath. As she turned to go into the house, he put out his hand to stop her.

"I'm going to drive you over, Matt," he whispered.

She replied in a low voice, "I think Zeena wants me to go with Jotham."

"I'm going to drive you over," he repeated. She went into the kitchen without answering.

At dinner, Ethan could not eat. If he lifted his eyes, they rested on Zeena's pinched face. Zeena ate well. She said the mild weather made her feel better. She even gave Jotham more beans.

When the meal was over, Mattie went about her task of clearing the table and washing the dishes. Jotham moved toward the door. Turning around, he asked, "What time should I come 'round for Mattie?"

Ethan looked at Mattie. "You needn't come 'round. I'm going to drive her over myself."

He saw the rise of color in Mattie's cheeks. Then Zeena quickly raised her head. "I want you to stay here this afternoon, Ethan," his wife said. "Jotham can drive Mattie over."

Mattie glanced at him with pleading eyes. But he repeated, "I'm going to drive her over myself."

Zeena continued in the same tone. "I want you to stay and fix up that stove in Mattie's room before the girl gets here. It ain't been working right for a month now. The girl that's coming told me she was used to a house where they had a furnace."

"She better stay there then," he flung back at her. Turning to Mattie, he added in a hard voice, "You be ready by three, Matt. I've got business at Corbury."

Jotham had started for the barn. Ethan walked down after him, burning with anger. His head was throbbing, and a fog was in his eyes. He went about his task not knowing whose hands and feet were doing the job. It was not until he hitched the horse to the sleigh that he became aware of what he was doing.

It reminded him of the day he drove over to the Flats to pick up Mattie. It was little more than a year ago, on just such an afternoon. There was the feel of spring in the air. The horse nuzzled the palm of his hand in the same way. One by one, he remembered all the days since then. They rose up and stood before him.

He flung the bearskin into the sleigh, climbed to his seat, and drove up to the house. When he entered, the kitchen was empty. Mattie's bag and shawl lay ready by the door. He went to the foot of the stairs and listened. No sound reached him from above. He thought he heard someone moving about in his study. He pushed open the door. Standing near the table, he saw Mattie. She was wearing her hat and jacket.

She turned to him quickly. "Is it time?"

"What are you doing here, Matt?" he asked her.

She looked at him shyly. "I was just taking a look 'round, that's all," she answered.

They went back into the kitchen without speaking. Ethan picked up her bag and shawl.

"Where's Zeena?" he asked.

"She went upstairs right after dinner. She said she had those shooting pains again. She didn't want to be disturbed."

"Didn't she say goodbye to you?"

"No. That was all she said."

Ethan looked around the kitchen. In a few hours, he would be returning to it alone. He could not bring himself to believe that Mattie was standing there for the last time before him.

"Come on," he said almost hopefully. He opened the door and put her bag into the sleigh. Then he sprang to his seat and tucked the rug about her.

"We got lots of time for a good ride, Matt!" he cried. He felt her hand beneath the fur and pressed it into his. His face tingled, and he felt dizzy.

At the gate, instead of going toward Starkfield, he turned the horse to the right. Mattie sat silent. She showed no surprise. But after a moment, she said, "Are you going 'round by Shadow Pond?"

He laughed and answered, "I knew you'd know!"

She drew close to him under the bearskin. The lane passed into pine woods. In the afternoon sun, gentle blue shadows fell on the snow. As they turned into the breeze, a warm stillness seemed to drop from the branches. Here, the snow was so pure that the tracks of wood animals looked like lace.

Ethan drove on in silence till they reached a clearing in the woods. Then he stopped and helped Mattie get out of the sleigh. They passed between the pine trees, the snow breaking crisply under their feet. Soon, they came to a small frozen pond. A single hill, rising against the sun, threw a shadow across the pond's frozen surface. That shadow gave the pond its name. It was a shy, secret spot, full of the same sadness Ethan felt in his heart.

Ethan looked up and down the pebble beach till he saw a fallen tree trunk half-hidden in the snow. "There's where we sat at the picnic," he reminded her.

They had sat there at the church picnic last summer. Mattie had begged him to go with her, but he had refused. Instead, he went to the woods to cut down some trees. Toward sunset, coming down from the mountains, he saw Mattie with a group of young men. He was drawn to her and the others by the pond. When she saw him, her face lit up. She broke through the group and came to him with a cup in her hand. They had sat for a few minutes on the fallen log by the pond. Suddenly, she missed her gold locket. The young men searched for it, and it was Ethan who found it in the moss. That was all, but it was happiness enough for them.

"It was right there I found your locket," he said.

"I never saw anybody with such sharp eyes!" she answered.

She sat down on the tree trunk in the sun, and he sat down beside her.

"You were as pretty as a picture in that pink hat," he said.

She laughed with joy. "Oh, I guess it was that hat!" she replied.

They had never before spoken so openly. Ethan felt for a moment like a free man wooing[1] the girl he meant to marry. He looked at her hair and longed to touch it again. He wanted to tell her it smelled of the woods. But he had never learned to say such things.

---

1. **wooing** trying to get the love or attention of a chosen person

Suddenly, she rose to her feet. "We mustn't stay here any longer."

He continued to gaze at her as if in a dream. "There's plenty of time," he answered.

There were things he had to say to her before they parted. But he could not say them in that place of summer memories. He turned and followed her in silence to the sleigh.

They turned back to the Starkfield road. Under the open sky, the light was still clear. Cold red shone on the eastern hills. The sky faded, leaving the earth more alone.

Ethan said, "Matt, what do you plan to do?"

She did not answer at once. "I'll try to get a job in a store."

"You know you can't do that. The bad air and the standing all day nearly killed you before."

"I'm a lot stronger than I was before I came to Starkfield."

"And now you're going to throw away all the good it's done you!"

There seemed to be no answer to this. They drove on for a while without speaking. Every spot they passed reminded Ethan of the time spent with Mattie.

"Isn't there any of your father's folks that could help you?"

"There isn't any of them I would ask."

He lowered his voice to say, "You know there's nothing I wouldn't do for you if I could."

"I know there isn't."

"But I can't."

She was silent. He felt a slight tremble in her shoulder against his.

"Oh, Matt," he broke out, " if I could have gone with you now, I would have done it!"

She turned to him, pulling a scrap of paper from her breast. "Ethan, I found this," she stammered. It was the letter to his wife he was writing the night before in his study. He had forgotten to destroy it.

"Matt," he cried, "if I could have done it, would you?"

"Oh, Ethan, Ethan! What's the use?" With a sudden movement, she tore the letter in shreds. It fluttered in the snow.

"Tell me, Matt! Tell me!" he begged her.

She was silent for a moment. Then she answered in such a low tone, he had to stoop his head to hear her. "I used to think of it sometimes, on summer nights, when I couldn't sleep."

His heart jumped with the sweetness of it. "As long ago as that?"

She answered, "The first time was at Shadow Pond."

"Was that why you gave me my coffee before the others?"

"I don't know. Did I? I was really sad when you wouldn't go to the picnic with me. And then when I saw you coming down the road, I thought maybe you came that way on purpose. That made me glad."

They were silent again. They had reached the point where the road went by Ethan's mill. The darkness came upon them. It dropped like a black veil from the heavy pine branches.

"I'm tied hand and foot, Matt. There isn't a thing I can do," he began again.

"You must write to me sometimes, Ethan."

"Oh, what good will writing do? I want to put my

hand out and touch you. I want to do for you and care for you. I want to be there when you're sick and when you're lonesome."

"You mustn't think those thoughts."

"You won't need me, you mean? I suppose you'll marry!"

"Oh, Ethan!" she cried.

"You don't know how it is you make me feel, Matt. I'd almost rather have you dead than married to someone else!"

"Oh, I wish I was, I wish I was!" she sobbed.

The sound of her weeping shook him out of his dark anger. He felt ashamed.

"Don't talk that way," he whispered.

"Why shouldn't we, when it's true? I've been wishing it every minute of the day."

"Matt! You be quiet! Don't you say it."

"There's never anybody been good to me but you."

"Don't say that either. I can't even lift a hand for you!"

"Yes, but it's true just the same."

They had reached the top of the hill. Starkfield lay below them in the twilight. A cutter passed them in a joyous flutter of bells. They looked straight ahead with stiff faces. As they drew near the end of the village, they heard the cries of children with sleds.

"I guess this will be their last coast for a day or two," Ethan said, looking at the clear sky.

Mattie was silent. He added, "We were to have coasted last night."

Still she did not speak. "Ain't it funny? We haven't coasted together but just that once last winter," he continued.

Finally, she answered. "It wasn't often I got down to the village."

"That's so," he said.

They had reached the top of the Corbury road. Between the white church and the black curtain of the Varnum spruces, they could see the empty slope below them. Not a single sled stretched across its banks. Something made Ethan say, "How would you like to coast down now?"

She forced a laugh. "Why, there isn't time!"

"There's all the time we want. Come along!" His one desire was to delay the moment of turning the horse back to the Flats.

"But the girl! She'll be waiting at the station."

"Well, let her wait. You'd have to if she didn't. Come!"

His commanding voice seemed to calm her. He jumped out of the sleigh, and she let him help her. "But there isn't a sled 'round anywheres," was all she could say.

"Yes, there is! Right over there under the spruces."

He caught Mattie's hand and drew her to the sled. She seated herself. He took his place behind her. She was so close that her hair brushed his face. "All right, Matt?" he called out.

She turned her head to say, "It's dreadfully dark. Are you sure you can see?"

He laughed. "I could go down this coast with my eyes tied shut!" She laughed with him at his boldness. Despite his boast, he sat still a moment. He strained his eyes down the long hill. It was the most difficult hour of the evening to see. The sky was fading into a blur with the coming darkness.

"Now!" he cried.

The sled started. They flew on through the dusk down the hill. They gathered speed as they went, with the air singing by like an organ. Mattie sat perfectly still until they reached the bend at the foot of the hill. There, the big elm thrust out a deadly elbow. Ethan felt her shrink a little closer to him.

"Don't be scared, Matt!" he cried. They spun past the tree and flew down the second slope. When they reached the level ground beyond it, he heard her give a joyful laugh. They jumped off the sled and started to walk back up the hill. Ethan dragged the sled with one hand and passed the other through Mattie's arm.

"Were you scared I'd run into the elm?" he asked with a boyish laugh.

"I told you I'm never scared with you," she answered.

"It *is* a tricky place, though," he boasted. "The least swerve, and we'd never come up again. But I can measure distances exactly, always could."

She whispered, "I always say you've got the surest eye."

Deep silence had fallen with the dusk. They leaned on each other without speaking. Every step he took, Ethan said to himself, "It's the last time we'll ever walk together."

When they got to the top of the hill next to the church, he asked her, "Are you tired?" She answered breathing quickly, "It was perfect!"

Ethan guided her toward the Norway spruces. "I guess this sled must be Ned Hale's. I'll leave it where I found it." He walked toward the Varnum gate and rested the sled against the fence. Suddenly, he felt Mattie close to him among the shadows.

"Is this where Ned and Ruth kissed each other?" she whispered breathlessly. Then she flung her arms about him. Her lips searched for his. They swept over his face. He held her fast in the joy of surprise.

"Goodbye," she stammered and kissed him again.

"Oh, Matt, I can't let you go!" he cried.

She freed herself from his arms. He heard her sobbing. "Oh, I can't go either!" she cried. "Matt! What will we do? What will we do?"

They clung to each other's hands like children. Her body shook with sobs. Through the stillness, they heard the church clock striking five.

"Oh, Ethan, it's time!" she cried.

He drew her back to him. "Time for what? You don't suppose I'm going to leave you now?"

"If I miss my train, where will I go?"

"Where are you going if you catch it?"

She stood silent, her hands lying cold in his.

"What's the good of either of us going anywhere without the other one now?" he said.

Suddenly, she threw her arms around his neck and pressed her wet cheek against his face. "Ethan! Ethan! I want you to take me down again!"

"Down where?"

"The hill. Right now. So we'll never come up anymore."

"Matt! What on earth do you mean?"

She put her lips against his ear. "Right into the big elm. You said you could. So we'd never have to leave each other any more."

"Why, what are you talking about? You're crazy!"

"I'm not crazy. But I will be if I leave you."

"Oh, Matt, Matt," he groaned.

"Ethan, where will I go if I leave you? I don't know how to get along alone. You said so yourself just now. Nobody but you was ever good to me. And there will be that strange girl in the house. She'll sleep in my bed. Just where I used to lay nights and listen to hear you come up the stairs."

Her words were like fragments torn from his heart. With them came the hated vision of the house he was going back to. He thought of the stairs he would have to go up every night, and the woman who would wait for him there. He thought of the sweetness of Mattie's words. Knowing she felt the same way, too, made returning to the other life unbearable.

Her begging still came to him between short sobs, but he no longer heard what she was saying. Her hat had slipped back. He was stroking her hair. At last, he found her mouth. They seemed for a moment to be by the pond together in the burning August sun. But when his cheek touched hers, it was cold and full of weeping. He saw the road to the Flats under the night and heard the whistle of the train up the line. The spruces covered them in blackness and silence. Ethan and Mattie looked as though they were in underground coffins. He thought to himself, "Perhaps it will feel like this. And afterwards, I won't feel anything."

"Come," Mattie whispered, tugging at his hand.

He pulled the sled out. The slope below them was empty. All Starkfield was at supper. Not a person crossed the open space in front of the church. He strained his eyes through the dimness. They seemed less sharp than usual.

He took his seat on the sled, and Mattie instantly

sat in front of him. Then suddenly, he sprang up again.

"Get up," he ordered her.

"No, no, no!" she cried.

"Get up!"

"Why?"

"I want to sit in front."

"No, no! How can you steer in front?"

"I don't have to. We'll follow the track. Get up! Get up!" he urged her. But she kept on repeating, "Why do you want to sit in front?"

"Because I want to feel you holding me," he stammered and dragged her to her feet.

The answer seemed to satisfy her. She did what he asked. He bent down and placed the runners carefully in the grooves worn by preceding coasters. She waited while he seated himself with crossed legs in the front of the sled. Then she sat behind him and placed her arms around him. Her breath on his neck made him tremble again. She was right, he thought to himself. This was better than parting. He leaned back and drew her mouth to his.

They started down the hill. Halfway down, there was a sudden drop, then a rise, and after that another long drop. It seemed to him as if they were flying indeed, flying far up into the cloudy night, with Starkfield below them. . . . Then, the big elm shot up ahead, lying in wait for them at the bend of the road. He said between his teeth, "We can fetch it; I know we can fetch it."

As they flew toward the tree, Mattie pressed her arms tighter around him. Her blood seemed to be in his veins. Once or twice, the sled swerved a little under them. He slanted his body to keep it headed for the elm. He kept repeating to himself again and again, "I know we can fetch it."

The big tree loomed bigger and closer. As they neared it, he thought, "It's waiting for us. It seems to know." But suddenly his wife's face, with its twisted lines, seemed to appear before him. He made a quick movement to brush it aside. The sled swerved, but he straightened it again. There was a last instant when the air shot past him like millions of fiery wires. And then the elm. . .

The sky was still dark, but looking straight up, he saw a single star. He thought it might be Sirius, but the effort tired him too much. He closed his heavy lids and thought that he would sleep. . . . In the stillness, he heard a little animal twittering[2] somewhere nearby under the snow. It made a small frightened *cheep* like a field mouse. He wondered if it were hurt. Then he understood it must be in pain—pain so bad that it felt like it was shooting through his own body.

He tried to roll over toward the sound. He stretched out his left arm across the snow. Now it was as though he felt rather than heard the twittering. It seemed to be under his palm, which rested on something soft and springy. The thought of the animal suffering was unbearable to him. He struggled to lift himself but couldn't. Something seemed to be lying on him. He continued to feel about with his left hand. He thought he might get hold of the little creature and help it. All at once, he knew that the soft thing he had touched was Mattie's hair. His hand was on her face.

---

2. twittering chirping sounds, one after the other

He dragged himself to his knees. She moved with him as he moved. His hand went over and over her face. He felt that the twittering came from her lips.

He got his face down close to hers. He put his ear to her mouth. In the darkness, he saw her eyes open and heard her say his name.

"Oh, Matt, I thought we'd fetched it," he moaned. Far off, up the hill, he heard the horse whinny. He thought, "I ought to be getting him his feed. . . ."

Epilogue

The droning voice stopped as I entered Frome's kitchen. Of the two women sitting there, I could not tell whose voice it had been.

One of them raised her tall, bony figure from her seat. She did not even glance in my direction. She went about, instead, preparing the meal that Frome's absence had delayed. A sloppy calico dress hung from her shoulders. Wisps of thin gray hair were pulled away from her high forehead, and they were fastened in the back by a broken comb. Her pale eyes revealed nothing. Her narrow lips were the same sallow[1] color as her face.

The other woman was much smaller. She sat huddled in an armchair near the stove. When I came in, she turned her head toward me, but her body did not move. Her hair was as gray as the other woman's, and her face was as pale. Under her shapeless dress, her body was limp and motionless. Her dark eyes had the bright witch-like stare that disease of the spine sometimes gives.

Even for that part of the country, the kitchen was a poor-looking place. The furniture was the roughest kind. A broken milk jug had been placed on a greasy, wooden table that was marked with knife cuts. Two chairs with straw seats and an unpainted dresser stood against the bare walls.

"My, it's cold here! The fire must be almost out," Frome said. He glanced about with sorry eyes as he followed me in.

---

1. **sallow** a sickly, pale-yellow color

The tall woman moved away from us toward the dresser. She didn't seem to notice. But the other, from her seat, answered complainingly. She said in a high, thin voice, "It's only been started this very minute. Zeena fell asleep and slept ever so long. I thought I'd be frozen stiff before I could wake her up and get her to 'tend to it."

I knew then that it was this woman who had been speaking when we entered.

The other woman was just coming back to the table. She carried the remains of a cold mince pie in a broken dish. She appeared not to hear the complaint brought against her.

Frome looked at me and said, "This is my wife, Mis' Frome." After another moment, he turned toward the figure in the armchair. "And this is Miss Mattie Silver. . . ."

Mrs. Hale, kind soul, had thought I was lost in the Flats and buried under a snowdrift. When I returned safely the next morning to her house, she was delighted to see me. She and her mother were amazed to learn that Ethan Frome's old horse had made it through the worst blizzard of the winter. They were even more surprised to hear that Ethan had taken me in for the night.

"Well," Mrs. Hale said, "in such a storm I suppose he had to take you in. I believe you're the first stranger to set foot in that house for over twenty years. He's that proud. He don't even like his oldest friends to go there. I don't know as any do, except myself and the doctor."

"You still go there, Mrs. Hale?" I asked.

"I used to go a good deal after the accident, when I was first married. But after awhile, I got to think it made them feel worse to see us. And then one thing and another came, and my own troubles. I usually drive over there 'round about New Year's and once in the summer. Only I try to pick a day when Ethan isn't there. It's bad enough to see the two women sitting there. But *his* face when he looks 'round that bare place just kills me. You see, I can remember what it was like in his mother's day, before their troubles."

Her mother, by this time, had gone up to bed. Mrs. Hale and I were sitting alone, after supper, in the parlor. I guessed she had kept silent all these years because she had been waiting for someone who had seen what she alone had seen. I waited for her trust in me to build. Then I said, "Yes, it's pretty bad, seeing all three of them there together."

She drew her brows into a frown of pain. "It was just awful from the beginning. I was here in the house when they were carried up. They laid Mattie Silver in the room you're staying in. She and I were great friends. She was to have been my bridesmaid in the spring. When she came to, I went up to her. She didn't know much till the morning. Then, all of a sudden, she woke up just like herself. She looked straight at me out of her big eyes, and said . . . Oh, I don't know why I'm telling you all this," Mrs. Hale broke off, crying.

She took off her glasses and wiped the tears from them. She put them on again with a shaking hand. "The next day, everyone knew that Zeena Frome had sent Mattie off in a hurry because she had a hired girl coming. The folks here could never figure why Mattie and Ethan had been coasting that night. They were supposed to be on their way to the Flats to catch the train."

She continued, "I never knew myself what Zeena thought. I don't to this day. Nobody knows Zeena's thoughts. Anyhow, when she heard of the accident, she came right in and stayed with Ethan at the minister's. That's where they carried him afterwards. And as soon as the doctors said that Mattie could be moved, Zeena sent for her. She took her straight back to the farm."

"And Mattie's been there ever since?"

Mrs. Hale answered simply. "There was nowhere else for her to go." My heart tightened at the thought of their hard, poor lives.

"Yes, there she's been," Mrs. Hale continued. "Zeena's done for her and done for Ethan as good as she could. It was a miracle, considering how sick she was. But she seemed to get right up when the need came. Not that she ever stopped doctoring herself. She's had sick spells right along, but she's had the strength to care for those two for over twenty years. And before the accident came, she thought she couldn't even care for herself."

Mrs. Hale paused for a moment. I remained silent, trying to picture what it had been like for the three of them. "It's horrible for them all," I murmured.

"Yes. It's pretty bad. And they ain't easy people either. Mattie *was* easy before the accident; I never knew a sweeter nature. But she's suffered too much. That's what I always say when folks tell me how she's soured. And Zeena, she was always cranky. She does get along with Mattie now. I've seen that myself. But sometimes, the two of them get going at each other. Then, Ethan's face would break your heart. When I see that, I think it's *him* that suffers most. Anyhow, it ain't Zeena, because she ain't got the time.

"It's a pity, though." Mrs. Hale ended, sighing. "They're all shut up there in that one kitchen. In the summer, on pleasant days, they move Mattie into the parlor or out in the yard. That makes it easier. But in winter, there's the fires to be thought of. And there ain't a dime to spare up at the Fromes'."

Mrs. Hale drew a deep breath, seeming to feel relieved that she had broken her silence after all these years. I thought she had no more to say. But suddenly, she took off her glasses and leaned toward me across the table. She lowered her voice. Then she said, "There was one day, about a week after the accident, when they all thought Mattie wouldn't survive. Well, I say it's a pity she *did*. I said it right out to our minister once, and he was shocked at me. But he wasn't with me that morning when she first came to. And I say, if she had died, Ethan might have had a decent life. The way they are now, I don't see there's much difference between the Fromes up at the farm and the Fromes down in the graveyard. Except that down in the graveyard, they're all quiet, and the women have to hold their tongues."

REVIEWING YOUR READING

PROLOGUE

FINDING THE MAIN IDEA

1. The main idea of the Prologue is that Ethan
   (A) is poor (B) had an accident (C) seldom speaks (D) has had only trouble all his life.

REMEMBERING DETAILS

2. The narrator learns that the"smash-up" occurred
   (A) only a year before (B) 10 years before (C) after Ethan was married (D) 24 years before.

3. The narrator meets Ethan because
   (A) he goes to the post office (B) he owes him money
   (C) there's a storm (D) Denis Eady's horses fell ill.

DRAWING CONCLUSIONS

4. Ethan is a "ruin of a man" because
   (A) his wife left him (B) he had a "smash-up" (C) he can't talk (D) he has no money.

5. Ethan invites the narrator into his home because
   (A) the horse is injured (B) they're too tired to go on in the storm (C) he wants him to see his house (D) he wants a friend.

IDENTIFYING THE MOOD

6. When Ethan drives the narrator to Corbury Junction, the mood is one of
   (A) coldness (B) silence (C) loneliness (D) all of these.

THINKING IT OVER

7. What do you think Harmon Gow means when he says, "Guess he's been in Starkfield too many winters. Most of the smart ones get away." What is Starkfield like in the winter? Why would people want to "get away?" Give reasons to support your answer.

CHAPTER 1

FINDING THE MAIN IDEA

1. This chapter is mainly about
   (A) Ethan and Denis Eady (B) the church dance (C) Ethan's feelings for Mattie (D) Ethan's marriage.

REMEMBERING DETAILS

2. Mattie Silver has been living with the Fromes for
   (A) one year (B) several years (C) all her life (D) none of these.
3. Ethan likes Mattie so much that he
   (A) does housework for her (B) shaves every day (C) shows her stars in the sky (D) all of these.

DRAWING CONCLUSIONS

4. When Ethan sees Mattie dancing with Denis Eady, his mood is one of
   (A) anger (B) sadness (C) jealousy (D) all of these.

USING YOUR REASON

5. Zeena is described as a "burden" because
   (A) she is ugly (B) she is sickly (C) she keeps to herself (D) none of these.

THINKING IT OVER

6. Why does Ethan like Mattie Silver so much? What do they share together? Give examples from the chapter to support your answer.

CHAPTER 2

FINDING THE MAIN IDEA

1. This chapter is mainly about
   (A) Ethan's fight with Denis (B) Ethan's walking Mattie home (C) Ethan's promise to Mattie (D) the missing key.

REMEMBERING DETAILS

2. Mattie tells Ethan that Ned Hale and Ruth Varnum
   (A) are engaged (B) are leaving town (C) were killed in a bad accident (D) decided not to get married.
3. Ethan promises to take Mattie the next night
   (A) dancing (B) sledding (C) to Bettsbridge (D) for a walk.

DRAWING CONCLUSIONS

4. Ethan asks Mattie if she will be leaving because
   (A) he wants her to go (B) he wants her to work harder
   (C) he wants her to stay (D) he wants her to marry Denis.

5. When Zeena opens the door, Ethan feels
   (A) glad (B) shocked and surprised (C) fearful (D) angry.

USING YOUR REASON

6. When Ethan sees a cucumber vine dangling from his porch, it
   reminds him of
   (A) holiday decorations (B) his farm (C) death (D) happy
   times at home.

THINKING IT OVER

7. At the end of the chapter, why do you think Ethan does not
   want Mattie to see him following Zeena upstairs to their bedroom? Give reasons to support your answer.

CHAPTER 3

FINDING THE MAIN IDEA

1. The most important event in this chapter is that
   (A) Ethan cuts the lumber (B) Zeena plans a trip (C) Zeena
   finds fault with Mattie (D) Ethan tells Mattie he loves her.

REMEMBERING DETAILS

2. An orphan at twenty years of age, Mattie was left with
   (A) no money (B) fifty dollars from the sale of her piano
   (C) a small inheritance (D) only the clothes on her back.

DRAWING CONCLUSIONS

3. Ethan dislikes Zeena's trips to the doctors because
   (A) she stays away a long time (B) he has to care for the farm
   himself (C) she buys expensive medicines (D) she spends too
   much money on things for the house.

USING YOUR REASON

4. This time, Ethan is glad Zeena is going away because
   (A) he won't have to drive her (B) he can spend the night out
   with Jotham Powell (C) he can spend the night alone
   (D) he can spend the night alone with Mattie.

THINKING IT OVER

5. What do you predict about Ethan and Zeena's marriage? How does Ethan treat Zeena? How does Zeena treat Ethan? What can you conclude about their relationship? Give examples to support your answer.

CHAPTER 4

FINDING THE MAIN IDEA

1. This chapter is mainly about
    (A) Zeena's leaving on her trip (B) Hale's giving Ethan the money (C) Mattie and Ethan's eating supper together
    (D) Ethan's hauling the lumber.

REMEMBERING DETAILS

2. Zeena had come to the Frome house to
    (A) do household chores (B) get away from Stamford
    (C) nurse Mrs. Frome (D) visit with Ethan.
3. The pickle dish is broken by
    (A) Ethan (B) Mattie (C) the cat (D) Ethan and Mattie together.

DRAWING CONCLUSIONS

4. Ethan married Zeena because
    (A) he was thankful to her for taking care of his mother
    (B) he was lonely after his mother's death (C) she was a skillful housekeeper (D) all of these.

USING YOUR REASON

5. Mattie is upset over the broken pickle dish because
    (A) she feels sorry for Zeena (B) she loved the dish (C) she took the dish without permission (D) none of these.

THINKING IT OVER

6. Why do Ethan and Mattie want to prevent Zeena from finding out about the broken pickle dish? What might the broken dish reveal to Zeena about them? Give reasons to support your answer.

CHAPTERS 5 AND 6

FINDING THE MAIN IDEA
1. The best title for Chapter 5 is
   (A) An Evening Together (B) Mattie and Ethan (C) Zeena's Trip (D) The Loves and Quarrels of Starkfield.

REMEMBERING DETAILS
2. After supper, Mattie sits in her chair
   (A) reading (B) sewing (C) petting the cat (D) none of these.
3. In Chapter 6, Ethan finally gets the glue from
   (A) Denis Eady (B) Jotham Powell (C) Widow Homan (D) none of these.

DRAWING CONCLUSIONS
4. In Chapter 5, when Mattie says the word "married," a pang goes through Ethan because
   (A) he loves her (B) he fears she will marry Denis Eady (C) he doesn't want her to leave (D) all of these.

USING YOUR REASON
5. The cat is a reminder that Zeena is gone because it
   (A) bothers Ethan (B) sleeps in front of the stove (C) sleeps in Zeena's chair (D) is greedy.

IDENTIFYING THE MOOD
6. As Chapter 5 begins, the *main* mood is one of
   (A) happiness (B) warmth and peace (C) excitement (D) loneliness.

THINKING IT OVER
7. In Chapter 6, Ethan has a plan, but "everything goes wrong." What does this tell you about Ethan? Give reasons to support your answer.

CHAPTER 7

FINDING THE MAIN IDEA
1. This chapter is mainly about
   (A) Ethan and Zeena's arguing (B) Zeena's plan to send Mattie away (C) the pickle dish (D) Mattie's fighting back.

REMEMBERING DETAILS

2. When Zeena returns home, she tells Ethan that the doctor said
(A) she needs an operation (B) she has "complications"
(C) she has "troubles" (D) all of these.

DRAWING CONCLUSIONS

3. Zeena has hired a new girl because
(A) Mattie doesn't help her enough (B) she's jealous of
Mattie (C) the doctor told her to (D) all of these.

USING YOUR REASON

4. Zeena is angry over the pickle dish because
(A) Ethan broke it (B) Ethan lied about the cat breaking it
(C) she loves it more than anything in the world (D) Mattie
broke it.

THINKING IT OVER

5. In your opinion what are Mattie's choices, given her experience and skills? Where will she go? What will she do? Give reasons to support your answers.

CHAPTER 8

FINDING THE MAIN IDEA

1. The best title for this chapter is
(A) Ethan and Mattie Leave (B) Ethan's Last Hope
(C) The Letter (D) Mrs. Hale Helps.

REMEMBERING DETAILS

2. In his study, Ethan writes a letter to
(A) Mattie (B) his relatives (C) Zeena (D) Daniel Byrne.

3. Ethan dreams of going with Mattie to
(A) Starkfield (B) Bettsbridge (C) the West (D) Stamford.

DRAWING CONCLUSIONS

4. Ethan believes that his last hope is to
(A) convince Zeena to let Mattie stay (B) divorce Zeena
(C) find a job for Mattie (D) borrow money from the Hales.

USING YOUR REASON

5. At the end of the chapter, Ethan decides he can't leave Zeena because
    (A) she is too sick and can't take care of herself (B) he feels sorry for her (C) he doesn't have enough money (D) all of these.

THINKING IT OVER

6. Why do you think Ethan decides not to ask Mr. Hale for money? What does this show you about Ethan's character? In your opinion, does he make the right decision? Give reasons to support your answer.

CHAPTER 9

FINDING THE MAIN IDEA

1. The most important event in this chapter is that
    (A) Mattie leaves (B) Ethan drives Mattie to town (C) there is an "accident" (D) Zeena lets Mattie stay.

REMEMBERING DETAILS

2. Ethan and Mattie crash into
    (A) a snow bank (B) an elm tree (C) Shadow Pond (D) a spruce tree.

DRAWING CONCLUSIONS

3. Ethan stops at Shadow Pond because
    (A) he wants to find Mattie's locket (B) it is Mattie's and his secret spot (C) he is tired and needs to rest (D) he wants to recall the feelings he had for Mattie there the previous summer.

USING YOUR REASON

4. Ethan may have decided to drive Mattie to Corbury himself
    (A) because he wanted her to be safe (B) so he could spend some extra time with her (C) so they could run away to the West (D) because he was planning to take her coasting.

THINKING IT OVER

5. What important decision do Ethan and Mattie make in this chapter? What other choices do they have? Give reasons to support your answers.

EPILOGUE

FINDING THE MAIN IDEA

1. When he enters Ethan's house, the narrator learns that the voice he hears is
   (A) Zeena's voice (B) the voice of a neighbor (C) Mattie's voice (D) Mrs. Hale's voice.

REMEMBERING DETAILS

2. The person who tells the narrator about the accident is
   (A) Mrs. Varnum (B) Jotham (C) Mrs. Hale (D) Mr. Hale.

DRAWING CONCLUSIONS

3. From the description of the smaller woman, we can conclude that she is
   (A) lazy (B) mean (C) sick (D) crippled.

4. From the description of the kitchen, we can conclude that the Fromes are very
   (A) poor (B) messy (C) lazy (D) busy with other things.

USING YOUR REASON

5. The fact that Zeena can take care of Ethan and Mattie right after the accident may suggest that
   (A) her health suddenly improved (B) she's very brave (C) she wasn't very sick to begin with (D) none of these.

USING YOUR IMAGINATION

6. Mrs. Hale tells the narrator that no one knows Zeena's thoughts. What do you imagine Zeena thinks about after the accident? Why do you think she takes Mattie in?

THINKING IT OVER

7. Mrs. Hale says that she thinks Ethan suffers the most. Do you agree? Give reasons to support your answer.